INFIDELS

INFIDELS

A Novel

Abdellah Taïa

Translated by Alison L. Strayer

Seven Stories Press
NEW YORK / OAKLAND

Seven Stories Press
140 Watts Street
New York, NY 10013
sevenstories.com

Library of Congress Cataloging-in-Publication Data

Taïa, Abdellah, 1973–
   [Infidèles. English]
   Infidels : a novel / Abdellah Taïa ; translated by Alison L. Strayer. --
Seven Stories Press first edition.
      pages cm
   ISBN 978-1-60980-680-4 (hardcover)
   ISBN 978-1-60980-806-8 (paperback)
   1. Mothers and sons--Fiction. 2. Morocco--Social conditions--Fiction. I.
Strayer, Alison L., translator. II. Title.
   PQ3989.2.T2716413 2016
   843'.92--dc23

                              2015029678

Printed in the United States of America

9 8 7 6 5 4 3 2 1

I. Soldiers

1

NOBODY WILL COME, MAMAN.
You know it, maman. It's too late. Or too early. The men don't come here anymore, and you know it. You know it. Isn't that true? Stop insisting, I don't want to do it anymore. Don't want anything to do with that ritual. We've been waiting a very long time. It's over. It's over. The last time we met up with a monster. He wanted to devour me. He did strange things to me. I told you. Remember? No? Really? Come on, we're going home. We're leaving, maman . . . We're leaving. The streets are empty, no one will see us, hurl insults and stones at us. And if anyone spits at you, I'll fight. I'll defend you. I won't run away. I've grown up. I can see I've grown up. I've learned to spit at people, too. Deep inside I remember everything. I'm not looking for trouble, but now if someone looks at me with evil eyes, eyes that cast spells, I know what to do. I spit. I stand my ground.
I don't look down, I face them down. I spit. I spit at all those people who despise us and pretend not to know you, maman. I spit. I spit. I spit with all my heart and soul. I spit as far as I can at the feet of my enemy and attacker, the bastard who won't let it drop but calls after me with his cheap remarks,

his tight-ass religious moralizing. I aim far, maman. I aim at the place where my attack will drive its point home. I inhale hard through my nose. I rake the bottom of my throat. I bring up all the half-dried snot from my nostrils onto my tongue. I hawk up all the filth from my lungs and mix it in my mouth with saliva. I get a big wad ready. I build up momentum. I attack. I launch my nuclear weapon. My gob of spit is so heavy, so sophisticated, it takes a while to land and explode in the face of my enemy, our enemies, maman. It's like in *Captain Majid* cartoons. The action happens in slow motion. My spit is suspended in midair. It'll stay that way forever. In the air. A serious threat to anyone who insults you, maman. I'll kill them all, blow them to pieces, pulverize them, wipe them off the face of the earth, of this world, this endless night, just with what comes out of my nose.

They say I'm dirty. You're dirty. I am the son of a dirty woman. The son of dirty Slima.

You're not dirty, maman. My Slima. I know that. You're not dirty. I swear to you. I swear.

Do you believe me?

You have to believe me.

I really know how to spit. Want me to prove it? I can. Right now. Spit all the way to that power pole. Do you want me to? I can.

You say nothing.

Spitting doesn't make me bad. Badly brought up. I was different from the start. Right from the beginning. Let me spit, and prove to you I've grown up. Let me show you how I can protect you.

Look at me. Look. Look.

You don't like me this way ... Don't worry. I'm growing up, but I'll never disown you. I understand. I accept. We don't have to change. This is how we are. How you are. Maman. Slima. I'm your son. Forever your son. Small, big, young, old, I'm your son.

I want to spit.

Let me. Let me.

It's what they deserve. All of them.

I spit on Samir and his mother. I spit on Hlima and his whole family. I spit on Youssef, Rachid, Fattah, Salim, and all the others. Friends from before. I spit on the whole soccer team of the El-Oued Khanez quarter and the team in Hay al-Inbiâth too. I spit on this city, Salé, and everyone who pretends they don't know you. I spit at the imam. I don't like him. He's a two-faced coward—dirty, very dirty. I don't want you to let him come to our house anymore. No more. Besides, he doesn't pay well. I spit in his face three times, no, five, the damn imam who can't even pray properly. They should send him back to primary school! He's ignorant. He needs to learn everything again. I spit at him hard, hard. I don't want you to see him again, not ever, maman. We don't need him, or his money, or his religion.

I spit at the neighbor Aisha and the black skillet she's hung in her ground floor window for so long. You can see it all the time from our house—that skillet, that curse. A year ago, you told me the meaning of the skillet, the message Aisha wants to send by hanging it there. Day after day and year after year, with the blackened skillet, so very black, she's been saying, "This is what you're worth, Slima, old slut. This is what I wish for you, to be burnt alive over the flames in this scorched pan! For you and your son to go to the Blackness forever, and soon! To be cursed forever in hell, on earth and in the Hereafter . . ."

I'm amazed. In the last few months, you haven't been fighting with Aisha. You gave up. She didn't. The black skillet is still there. A permanent insult. A constant reminder of our status in Hay al-Inbiâth. For the tens of thousands of people around us, we deserve our pariah status, our grim fate, because we do nothing to change it, break out of it. Maman, one day you'll be stoned to death by the very same people who creep to the house each night to ask for your forgiveness and a bit of pleasure.

You're dead. You don't exist anymore. You're evil. I'm the son of evil, of sin. That's what Aisha-the-curse calls me, "Son of evil." She always tells me to stay away from her two sons, not touch them or play with them. She says, "keep your evil to yourself and your mother Slima!" But I like her sons, and they knew everything about evil long before they met me. They're not afraid of evil.

Yes, I'm surprised. You have no more desire to fight Aisha or any other witch. Why? Can you tell me? Why? I'm growing. I may still seem small to you, but I've grown, Maman. Look at me. Look at me. I can fight for you. Avenge you. Spit day and night at Aisha and all the others, your "eternal enemies," you often say.

You're not answering. Why?

Are we going to wait here long? Until when? No one's coming. They don't come here anymore. They don't pass this way. Foreign men don't know our neighborhood now. They all go live in the Hay Salam district. That's where you'll have to go looking now, to lure them, talk to them, negotiate with them. Sing. Dance. Take off your clothes. Do you want us to go there? Do you need my help? Yes? No? Yes?

You're still not answering.

I'm tired of waiting. We're going back. We're going back, maman. I don't know if it's day or night. I don't know. I want to spit, spit, spit. I feel it coming up. You don't want me to, is that it? Maman. Answer, maman! Answer. Are you with me? Where are you?

The desire to live is slipping away. You feel it, like me. You see it, like me. And still you do nothing. You bring me here and we wait. But they don't come to this hammam now. They're all in Hay Salam. That's where we have to go. Away from those people who know us too well, know everything about you, more than I do—those people, those neighbors who look right through me. I can't stand it anymore. Let's go someplace else, maman. Let's go to Hay Salam and start over, from the beginning. I'm sure people will be nicer there. I'm sure.

Say something.

Do you hear me? Have you heard of Hay Salam? It's the new trendy area in Salé. I already love the name. Hay Salam. Salam. Peace. Peace at last, Maman. What do you think?

Say yes. It'll be good. A place where nobody knows you, yet. Say yes.

Say something! Talk!

I'm going. I don't want to wait here. The men are gone. They don't want me anymore here. The hammam's too dark and dirty. It's haunted. Old. All the nice Berber masseurs who worked here returned to their village in the back of beyond, near Taroudant. The watchman got sick. The bodies here aren't how they were before. They don't speak anymore, they've retreated into fear and solitude. Maman, we have to go. No one sees me here anymore. In just a year, I went from one hammam to the other. I assure you, I don't miss the women's side at all. A year isn't enough to learn to be a teenager, enter all those dramas cold, no transition. It wasn't easy on the men's side, with tall hairy strangers, terrifying and rarely gentle. You pushed me to do all that, cross that border, just let <u>it happen</u>. I trusted you. We came here. We waited. We found them quickly, very quickly. We even had plenty of choice. Men the way you like them. Docile. Strangely shy. You approached them. You spoke softly. You always knew the right words to pull them in, soften them up. Bring them to their knees.

"Sir, sir, please, could I entrust my son to you? To wash with you in the hammam? Would that be possible? My son's a nice boy. And I'm alone, without a man. This little boy is all I have. He's well-behaved, you'll see. Could you do that? Are you sure? It's not a nuisance? Everything is in this little bag. Everything. Cadum Shampoo. Black soap. *Ghassoul.* A glove for scrubbing. A small towel. A big towel. Clean clothes. And two tangerines. One is for you . . . Are you sure you don't mind? Sure? All right. Here are the 5 dirhams for the entrance fee. Here. Here, please, sir. I insist, I insist . . . You're already doing me a favor, taking him in, looking after him in the hammam. Here. Take the five dirhams. Here . . ."

They never took the money. They knew very well they'd be paid in another way later.

"Then come to my home after the hammam, for couscous. You'll come? My little boy will show you the way. Couscous . . . It's the least I can do . . ."

I always did as you told me. But I didn't like all the men you chose for me, and later for yourself. At first I couldn't care less. It's not like that now. I think we went through all the men of Hay Al-Inbiâth, maman.

Maybe I should go to the hammam alone this time. To this hammam, alone and for the last time.

I'm big.

Ten years old is big, isn't it?

What are you thinking about?

Do you want to know what happened inside with those men, before we arrived at the house for couscous? Do you want to come in with me this time?

Shall I tell you everything?

You already know everything about men?

I doubt it, maman, I doubt it.

Let me go. Let me go alone. The men are all gone. They've disappeared from this world, from this night without borders. They no longer exist here, on this side, with us, for you, for me. Give it up, maman.

Go, go, go home. Sleep. Forget. And wait for me. I'll come back a new person, stronger, smarter. I won't be your son anymore. I'll be your brother, your little brother.

I've been here in this boat with you from the beginning. I'll never leave you. We'll ride together till the end. Sing and dance. Love and sleep. Still eat, in spite of everything. Together all the way to God. Until the Last Night. All the way to paradise. We'll climb the stairs of heaven. I'll help you. I'll carry you. When you're old, I'll still be there for you, though everyone, all the others have cast you out. I'll talk to God, He will forgive us. God already accepts us as we are. He made us this way. In this condition. In this situation. We accept His decisions. We listen to His voice. You hear Him too, don't you?

Every night, he tells me to watch over you.

Every night, God loves us a little more.

The others crush us, prevent us from seeing the light; more and more, they shut us into a hell they first invented for themselves. But He, God, Allah, is not them, isn't like the image they made of Him.

God is in me. He's also in you. You're the one who gave me God. I know you also give Him to others, the men who come to our house, sleep at our house, eat with us, get undressed and dressed again at our house. You're the one who sees Him, more than me. Much more.

Do you hear me?

Do you understand me?

Are you with me?

Go home. Start getting ready for the move. We'll take only the essentials. Our clothes. Especially our clothes. We'll even take the most ragged ones that should be thrown in the trash. We won't give them to the poor or to strangers. They're our souls, you told me one day, young and old, in succession.

We'll keep our souls, maman.

Put them in green bags. Open the windows. Look at the sky. It's black, but that's just how it looks. The sky isn't black. We only see it that way.

Look at the sky for a long time, maman. It'll break open in the end. Explode.

I'll be back soon.

I'll be back soon.

I'll go back to the hammam alone. For the first time, alone. I'll get undressed. Take everything off. I'll be naked. Naked. NAKED. I'll be alone and naked. In the middle room, I'll scrub my own back. I'll blacken my own body with traditional soap. And I'll wait until the Angel without religion comes to cleanse me, give me new life. A new name.

For the last time, I'll remove the dirt from my body. My dead skin. My odors that have offended you for a year now. My nails that grow too quickly. Again and again, with no shampoo, I'll pour very hot water over my head. I won't be afraid. I'll hide my trembling deep inside. I'll stifle it. From now on, it would be indecent to let my fears and horrible images overwhelm me. Soon, hair will grow out of my body. Short hairs, soon very long. I know the process. I know how quick it will be. The hair on my body will take us to a new phase, a new era, maman.

You don't believe me?

Try. Look at me. I'm your son. The son of Slima. Better

than a son. You've told me everything. I've seen everything. I know your body by heart. I know how your skin moves, how it changes. Your voices are familiar. Your angels. Your djinns are my friends.

You have to let me go. Let me enter the hammam alone. Catch my death and my life. Leave childhood. And always, always be with you, by your side.

I promise. I swear.

I'm all you have, maman.

You're all I have, Slima.

I'll be another person, yours forever.

They'll pass through. Only pass through. Men of all ages. Sorcerers. Bad guys. Friends. Parents. Police. Politicians. Madmen. They all end up leaving. Freedom with you is not to their taste. It scares them. They don't know how to play. They don't want to let themselves go anymore. They don't like me. Apart from the muezzin and the postal official, none of them has ever looked at me.

We have to go. Maman. Maman Slima. We have to leave this place.

Hay Salam isn't far. But the sky is different there; the air is different.

The men are new.

There's a vegetable market every day.

Our past won't exist in Hay Salam. We'll write it the way we want to. Another story.

Our hammam there will be the Al-Baraka. It just opened. It exists. It has a more or less secret part, a family hammam. The whole family naked without shame, there together to change skin and even change sex. A hammam where we can both go. With everyone's blessings. You and I. We're a family, just you and me. That tradition has finally been imported here. I'm told it has been around a long time in other places. Fez. Wazzane. Meknes. Isn't that right, maman? You knew that, didn't you? Was it like that in your first country, Rhamna? Yes? No?

You don't want to answer.

You're being stubborn.

You don't want to let your clients down. To be adrift again, starting all over. Hungry. Panhandling. Working as a maid for the rich, the ruthless bourgeois.

I promise that won't happen, not now. I'm here. Hay Salam is rich. You won't have to suffer from competition. We won't have enemies. Aisha and her black skillet will be a just a bad memory. I'll grow up more free. I'll spit somewhere else. Never in front of you. I owe you that.

You're still young.

You're beautiful.

That is your fate.

Our fate.

I know it. I see that fate. I have to force it on you. I'm only ten. I've already been through a lot with you.

Your sounds. Our rituals. I'm not just ten. I'll talk from now on. I'll ask questions. You'll never have to reply.

Go home. Go home, maman.

Drink a glass of wine if you want. It'll revive you, warm you, help you listen to me, understand me at last. Let me go. See me for what I am.

I just turned ten.

The age of manhood.

It's like in the Egyptian movies on television. But this is reality. Moroccan reality. Hard. Bitter. Ruthless.

Ten, maman. A man, maman.

People won't forgive me anything now. They'll stop saying, "it's not his fault!"

The judgments are only just beginning. You can't protect me anymore. Scream for me. Fight with people to save me. Give and take blows for me.

That's all over.

I'm a man now.

I need to talk. Negotiate. Scam, charm, distract them. Rip them off. Suck them, maybe. Offer my backside if I have to. Hide my purity, my God. Hold my tongue about our secret bond. About who you are and who I am. About our road through the shadows. Our plans. The night voyage.

I'm going to do all that, maman.

I'm the man now.

I have a man's sex. It's revealing itself. Protruding. It's not afraid anymore.

Tonight, hair will sprout all over my body. My smell will change. My breath too. My nipples will harden. I'll sweat more. More than ever. More than you. Winter and summer.

Go home, maman Slima. Go home.

It's still nighttime. Night. We can sneak away. They won't know anything. Go home. Go.

That's an order.

I still want to laugh from time to time. With you. In spite of others.

I have to face it.

I have to go brave this nightmare. In the hammam. Alone. Alone.

Go home.

Please.

Go home.

Pack our suitcases.

I'll carry them.

I'll take your hand.

Go home.
I'll be back soon.
I'll just be an hour. No more.
An hour to find myself again.
An hour to talk to Him, man to man.
Go home.
I'll be back.
It will never be late.

2

I'M GOING TO DIE, my daughter. my little Slima.

I'm leaving.

Listen to me. I'm your mother. Memorize every word that comes out of my mouth.

Now my words are worth their weight in gold.

My time has run out. He's on his way. He's coming down. I see Him.

Listen to me, Slima, my little girl, my flesh, my legacy, my light, my final memory. Listen ... Listen ...

I still have a bit of strength to tell you what I have to say.

Get me something to drink. A big glass of water. And put in a mint leaf. Two leaves. Go. Run.

I'll keep talking to myself while I wait.

I beg You, slow down a little, go somewhere else, take other souls. Give me another hour, just an hour. I must talk to my daughter, pass on my knowledge, reveal all my secrets to her. I protected her for a long time, my darling little girl. I took her in, saved her from the street and its perils. I thought I could find another fate for her, another trade, another future, different from mine. But time passed quickly, very quickly, too quickly. I'm old. Old enough to leave, cross the river, give Him my hand. I didn't see it coming. I aged in one fell swoop. Just like that. All my strength left one summer morning. The day before, I was running in the streets and climbing stairs effortlessly. Salty, sweet, spicy—I ate it all. And then one morning, everything stopped. Closed in on me. I really didn't see it coming. I guided people and time. Now I'm at the bottom of time, and playing with a snake in spite of myself. He's the one who will take me. Your Messenger. But why a snake? Why not a sweet angel with wings? You can't do anything? That's all You have on hand at the moment? A snake for me to say goodbye with, cut my ties with?

I'm frightened.

You're back, Slima.

Let me look at you a moment. You're not a little girl anymore. You're becoming a woman. You've grown. You're taller than me now. Just as well.

Give me something to drink. That's the only thing I still long for. Water. With those little peppermint leaves. The taste of paradise.

Give it to me. That's all I'll take with me in the end. I want to leave cleansed, pure from the inside out.

Do you believe me, my daughter? Do you believe I was pure?

You don't know . . .

People have always given me another picture of myself. I'm perverse. The perverse old woman everyone needs. A bit of a witch. A bit of a doctor. A bit of a whore. The sex specialist.

They all came to me for help and they all turned their backs on me. That's how it goes. I've known it from the start. Ingratitude defines men. And women. But still I'm a little surprised. They moved out of the way when I passed. All at once. They said I wasn't a good Muslim. What do they know? I know

Islam better than anyone. I speak to God directly, no need for an intermediary. Those people don't know anything about anything.

They all dropped me. For years I waited in great solitude—in Tadla, near the city of Beni Mellal, my own country, my own region, in exile.

Contrary to what they said, I wasn't really old when I left. Barely forty.

I'd had enough of the hostility and rejection they constantly made me endure. I sold everything. I left the country. First I went to Casablanca to see my stepsister El-Batoule. But she'd just been married for the tenth time. Her new husband knew nothing, then, about my past or hers. She was trying to make herself over as a good submissive wife. I had no right to spoil her plans and drive away this rare husband who was also a good and proper Muslim, so it seemed. I didn't insist. She made it clear she couldn't have me come to stay. I understood. Instead of going north as I'd planned, I headed south. I came here to Rhamna. Marrakech isn't far. You know that, don't you? Only fifty kilometers.

I didn't know anyone in Rhamna. So I did what I do best—took refuge with a patron saint.

I went to the mausoleum of a local saint. One of many. There are plenty of them here. I went to the first who turned up on my route. I got out of the bus, dead tired. Disgusted by other people—by everything, in fact. But still the life in me yearned to express itself, to carry on through my forsaken body.

Like all abandoned women in this country, I lay down by the tomb of the saint. Our Protector. Instantly, a sense of peace came over me. I felt lighter. I traveled.

Day turned into night.

I slept and didn't sleep.

I told him everything. That's what he's there for, our saint.

To receive the words of people like me, rejected women like me.

I didn't choose that fate. I found myself inside it. All I did was take it on. I was pushed into it—that trade from another time. I may be one of the last of those women who help couples unite on their wedding night. After me, there will be no one but you, my daughter.

He listened to me say the same things a thousand times, tell the same story. About my life that no one wanted. My withered body. My hands that still knew how to guide, to take, and found nothing more to take. My knowledge. My songs. My rituals. Everything was going to be lost. Disappear forever. It was a second death, the most dreadful, the most unbearable. It was out of the question to accept it, subject myself a second time to this cruel fate. I chose none of it and yet I took it all on, accepted it all. I still wanted to honor the contract. Stay true, until the very end, to what had made me a pariah. A useful woman in great demand, and now a disgrace, a shadow—filth.

I still wanted to live. Despite others' cruelty, I wanted to keep breathing, walking, eating, devouring, casting spells. Teaching men how to use their sex. Revealing to women the techniques of pleasure. The secrets of their vaginas. I had a gift for that science. I hadn't forced myself. It's true that I'd been pushed toward the profession, but it was all inside me from the start. The science of sex, of sexes. The road to pleasure. The meeting. One body inside the other. One sex inside the other, deep inside.

Men know nothing.

Women are afraid.

You need to know that, Slima my daughter.

He, the saint, knew it only too well, of course. He understood my restlessness, my dismay. He saw the life in me still throbbing, untamed.

Life strong in my old woman's body. He saw beyond me, far beyond the mask I was forced to wear so people would let me be, just a little, give me a bit of peace.

The "bad woman." That's what they called me.

The saint, that night, told me I was not.

He repeated it three times.

"You're not a bad woman.

You're not a bad woman.

You're not a bad woman."

He rose from his grave.

He lay down beside me.

He held my hand. And he spoke to me.

"The night will never end. I'm giving you a little light for your final years. A child who will be your mirror, your walking stick, your feet, your double. Your blood. Better than your blood. A devotee. Your religion. A religion for just the two of you.

Sleep. Sleep. It will be night for a long time yet. The Chergui, from the east, is an evil wind. It will blow for a long time yet, to trouble the world.

Sleep. I won't let go of your hand anymore."

The saint's words are still alive in me. I'm dying and I can still hear them. I'm leaving and his voice comes back to me, beautiful, pure, welcoming.

He was the only one who ever helped me sleep in a different way. Who didn't judge me.

He showed me his heart.

When I woke up, you were sitting beside me. A little girl of five, maybe six. You looked at me.

The light was you.

I hadn't been dreaming. Night isn't made for dreams. Night is for finding the truth at last. Deciding everything. Accomplishing everything. Going to your fate alone. Coming back from it the same, but different.

I revived.

I didn't know anyone in Rhamna. I loved only two things in that village: red earth, blood mixed with dust, and the saint who had spoken to me.

I aimlessly wandered. I found myself in darkness. I communed. I freed myself without relinquishing anything. And you arrived.

I know nothing of you, my daughter.

Thanks to you, my life will go on.

Yours is forever linked to mine.

I'm leaving. In a moment it will be the end. But I know I'll continue with you, through you. You don't believe me? It doesn't matter. You'll see. Only a few months after I'm gone, all of me will come back to haunt you. My gestures. My voice. My neuroses. My tics. My hands that redraw the world. My shortness of breath. My mad dances. Even my vulgarity, my filthy words will come back to you. Every day. Just before sleep.

You won't be yourself except through these memories of me engraved in your mind and body in spite of yourself. You'll see. You'll discover that you'd only forgotten. Nothing leaves forever. You will live, my daughter. You'll be like me. You'll live for both of us. Woman. Two women in one. You'll feel my blood inside you. Will know it. It will flow through you. Your first mother left you, abandoned you at the saint's mausoleum. You were barely six months old. The visitors who passed through that sacred place, one after another, took care of you. The saint gave the order. You were six years old when he chose me as your second mother, your real mother. He saved me. You saved me.

I've always told you everything. Almost.

You didn't speak. You still don't speak. But your affection for me has never faded. You adopted me more than I adopted you. My bad temper never went away. You bore it without protest. I prevented you from going to school. You accepted it. From the age of seven, you took care of this house. You cleaned, you washed, you mopped the floor, you dusted, you polished all the walls and corners. I don't know where you got this obsession with cleanliness, your improbable liking for bleach. Not from me. Definitely not. You shopped for food every day. You cooked. And when necessary, you disappeared. You knew the customers didn't like to see you. You went up to the terrace and looked at the sky. I know. I saw you, I don't know how many times, merging with the sky, and you flew, my daughter, you flew, I swear. The sky loved you. Much more than I did, perhaps. Better than I.

You don't talk, Slima.

I don't think you'll ever talk.

Listen to my last words, then. My last secrets. Memorize everything that comes out of my mouth. Open your ears. Your memory. Your skin.

Gold. Jewelry first.

Next to Casablanca there's a town called Azemmour. Small. Poor. Incredibly beautiful. I lived there a little over a year. Now, when was that exactly? I'm losing my memory. Ah! It's coming back now. After my sister refused to let me stay with her and her husband in Casablanca, that's where I went first. I knew one great joy and one great tragedy there. I'll tell you about it. I'll tell you later. Don't forget the name of that city. Azemmour. That is where you'll go tomorrow, day after tomorrow at the latest. That is where you'll bury me. Do you understand? You have to do it. Bury my body in the cemetery of that city, next to the mausoleum of Saint Moulay Bouchaïb. Nowhere else.

Do you promise?

Swear to me. Swear, my daughter. My little Slima. My love. Give me your hand. Put the other on your heart.

Now, swear.

All I really love is that city, Azemmour, the saint Sidi Moulay Bouchaïb, and the river that talks back and forth with them. That river has a magnificent name. Oum Er-Rbia, the mother of Spring. Azemmour is the mouth of the river that flows through the land where I was born, where I grew up, Tadla near Beni Mellal. Azemmour is the *baraka*-water that meets the water from before, from Time eternal: the ocean, where everything on this earth comes from.

My daughter. I want you to live there. Drink that water. Swim in the Oum Er-Rbia. Go to the places I've been. Continue my story. Bring me justice. I'm not a bad woman.

Am I?

Am I, my dear little girl?

In Azemmour, you'll be unknown, foreign, as I was at first. You'll invent your freedom. They won't dare spit at you.

You're sixteen, Slima.

It's time for me to leave.

It's time for you to flee.

There, in the cemetery of Moulay Bouchaïb, you will build me a nice tomb. A red tomb. They'll tell you it's not allowed, that it's against our religion. Don't listen to them. Whatever you do, don't listen. I want a simple tomb, plain, no marble, and no decoration. But I want it to be red.

That is very important, my daughter. Red. Red as the earth of Rhamna.

Put your hand back on your heart.

Forty days after my death, you will build this tomb, this little mausoleum. During the night. Don't forget. At night. You will find a nice little mason. Young. Who knows how to read and write. Promise to give him what he wants: pleasure, sensual delirium, ecstasy. You'll direct him. So he'll carry out your orders, my orders, to the letter.

A simple tomb. I repeat. Simple. Red.

You will ask him to write my name: Saâdia Tadlaoui. My age: 80 years. I believe. The year of my death: 1970. The season of my death. Summer. My trade: *introductrice*.

1970. Summer. Red. Remember that date and those three instructions. It's 1970. Summer is burning everything up. Red is our final color, the one we keep forever.

That's all I want for this ceremony, for my return. No prayers—nothing. I only want your heart that still carries me inside it, strong and tender. No Koranic verses or Arabic poems. Nothing. Nothing else.

I want to go to heaven a virgin. With the name I gave myself. Saâdia. With the family name of the man I loved most, back in the village, Tadla. The man who never wanted me. To marry me. For his family, I could only ever be bad, a wicked woman forever. He couldn't go against his family. He turned out to be weak and timid, passive, despite his sex, which would have done a donkey proud. I left without asking for anything, without belittling or hurting him. I loved him sincerely, truly. I took his name. Tadlaoui. From Tadla. Our earth, his and mine.

I gave myself to him, opened myself, body, heart and soul. Everything in me is his. Living. Dead. I want to meet God and be with the man I love again, but in the way I want, not as others choose.

That is why it's important for you to do all this at night. For three nights.

The first night is for building my tomb.

The second is for writing, engraving my name, my book.

On the final night, you'll come back alone. The cement on the grave will have dried. The name and history will be set forever. And you can finally paint the tomb red. Paint me red.

The third night you will lie beside me. Do not sleep. Don't sleep, whatever you do. At a certain moment, something will be revealed to you. Another red tomb. Today, that tomb isn't red anymore. It will turn red again on the third night. I don't know exactly when. So don't sleep. Do not sleep. The tomb isn't far from mine. It will recover its color for barely fifteen minutes. No more. That is what I've been told. And you have to believe me. Anyway, you have no choice.

The other red tomb will shine.

You will go to it quickly.

You will dig. With your hands. Gently.

That is where I hid the gold, my jewelry. My treasure. My legacy.

That is where I buried your little brother.

You had a brother, Slima, my girl.

I understand you're shocked. That's your right.

He was barely two months old when he died.

I had him long before I met you at Rhamna.

I had him in my belly when I left my country, Tadla. But I didn't know it. He was the fruit of my love with the man of Tadla who didn't want to marry me. He was the father. Not another man. Do you believe me?

I was about forty. I realized I was pregnant when I arrived in Azemmour. I was astonished. A child at forty? Is that possible?

I knew no other woman who'd given birth at that age. A miracle! At the time, a woman was considered old at forty, good for nothing.

My sister refused to let me stay with her in Casablanca. I had to go somewhere else. Where? My feet guided me to Azemmour.

I hid there for a little under a year waiting for the pregnancy to come to term. I could have aborted. I know how. I've helped many women do it. But I didn't want to. That child was the fruit of love. He came from the man I still loved passionately, madly. I had to keep him.

Azemmour took me in without judgment, without treating me as an infidel.

Azemmour is a separate territory. A city from another time. Free and unbridled. I was able to give birth there, to a boy. Smile at him, give him my breast. Wash him, keep him warm. Calm and comfort him. Teach him little things.

But it didn't last long.

I slept. Too much. It was winter. I was completely exhausted. I slept much more than I should have. One morning when I woke up, he wasn't breathing. The little baby, your brother, wasn't breathing. His body was cold, his eyes open wider than usual.

I didn't cry. Don't judge me, please.

I felt a sort of relief.

All by himself that little child had understood the way things were. The world was already hurting him. Even I, without wanting to, had abandoned, killed him.

I didn't tell anyone.

People didn't really know me in Azemmour.

Alone, I buried him in the cemetery of St. Moulay Bouchaïb. I didn't pray for him. At the time, I too was somehow convinced that I was living in sin. This son, born out of wedlock, was the child of sin. One day, someone would spit in his face, make his life miserable with that insult, that narrow truth.

I hadn't even given him a name.

God didn't love him, of that I was sure.

I gave him to Life to look after. To Nature. The World after the world. Black stars, dead and so bright.

I put him in the ground without a shroud. I laid him in his grave with his baby clothes that still bore traces of me. Sweat, dried milk from my breasts. All I could give him was what I was, a shameful woman.

But a mother all the same.

Don't judge me, my little daughter.

It was night. I could only do it at night.

I dug with my hands. He was so little. His grave was easy to dig.

I laid him in that welcoming hole.

Tears were coming. To keep them away, I sang a Berber song I didn't understand. It came from another place, a life in the mountains I couldn't remember.

He was dead. But I was sure that he heard, was listening to me.

I'd never sung to him before. It was the first and last time.

A nocturnal lullaby.

The words in Berber took the baby back to ancestors I knew nothing about who would teach him everything. Guide him. Take care of him for me. Heal him. Love him. Talk to him in the first language. Berber. Lost. Forgotten. Neglected. Crushed. Hidden. But always true.

Before Arabic there is Berber. Before Morocco, Amazigh.

I don't remember covering the baby in earth. I was absent when it happened. It wasn't me who did it. I'm sure. Sure.

Forty days later, I returned to the cemetery at night. I built the tomb myself. And I painted it red.

I didn't write anything on the tombstone. I'm illiterate, my girl. And my baby had no name.

Hence the idea of distinguishing his grave from others with red.

You'll see. When the red returns to that little tomb, you'll be surprised and moved. You'll understand. You'll go to it naturally and sing for the little brother you never knew. The same Berber song. You haven't heard it. I never taught it to you. In front of the little mausoleum, the baby, alive again, will whisper the words and tell you where I hid the treasure. Next to his body. On the right side.

You will listen to him, Slima.

You will follow his orders, my girl.

And for once, you will open your mouth. You will speak. No. You'll sing. You'll travel along the same road, speak the same language as him, as me, as all of us.

Berber. That's what we are, Berbers. You'll see. You'll wake up. Berbers, always and forever.

You'll have two tombs at Azemmour. And the saint. Sidi Moulay Bouchaïb.

They'll be your family. Extended.

Don't forget to take care of us.

Don't forget the saint. Pay him a visit at least once every season. Give to the poor. To dishonored women.

The little treasure I'm leaving you isn't much. A belt. Ten *louises*. A chain and its *khamsa*. All gold. Do what you want with it. It will help you get settled, buy a little house in the old town. You'll be protected for a while. A year. Two years, maybe.

You are now sixteen.

Very soon you'll be eighteen.

You're not beautiful.

In Azemmour you will be.

I don't want you to become a little housemaid, a slave, a beggar. You won't need those people. Other people. They'll come to you, seeking your knowledge, your skills, your blessings. No marriage will be sealed without you, my girl.

You'll be an *introductrice*, like me.

Free, like me.

A queen. Not in the eyes of others, who are ignorant and will always see you as a prostitute. A queen, because you're the one who's decided what you will be.

You'll do what I do. You'll help both men and women. You'll bring them together at last. You'll introduce them into each other.

I told you earlier.

Men know nothing.

Women are afraid, and people do everything to keep them that way. Submissive. Fearful. Nice little ladies.

You will do good, my girl. They'll give you money, smile at you, and as soon as you're gone, they'll curse you.

It doesn't matter.

It really doesn't matter.

I will not die. Through you, I'll still be here on earth.

You'll take cocks in your hands. You'll open vaginas wide.

And to do that, you'll have to talk.

Here's how I did it.

Here's how you'll do it.

You'll be the only person allowed in the bridal chamber. It is the wedding night. Outside, everyone is celebrating. Dancing, drinking, singing, they easily drift into a trance. Wine and emotion are overflowing. Almost nobody in the two families knows you're there on the bed with the couple about to be joined. It is you who will unite them. Put one sex in the other. For the first time. He won't be able to get hard. She'll be petrified and won't want to undress. The husband, you'll have to arouse with filthy words, wild words from the street.

You'll have to remove the bride's clothing yourself. You'll be gentle, violent. You have to be quick. The newlyweds' mothers are waiting anxiously behind the door. They're not singing. They're praying.

The bride must be a virgin. That's how it goes. This is no time for discussion. It's not your role to ask questions. Blood must flow. That's all anyone is waiting for, the proof of that fictitious purity.

It's up to you.

You'll have to cheat. Tell the husband to close his eyes. Explain that it's very important. Promise him a thousand pleasures. It's not the end of the world. Blood can flow from anywhere. Thighs, arms, calves. You have to be ready to cheat and be quick about it. And it will be necessary almost every time.

First you'll defend your sisters—women. Even when they declare war on you, you won't betray them on their wedding night. Most arrive at this moment without being virgins. That's how it goes. It's your job to make sure blood flows onto the white sheet that will be proudly displayed for friends and enemies alike. You'll see. You already know the earth will stop turning if we don't give people the illusory proof that women are faithful, brainless, docile things who will never belong to themselves.

You'll carry each woman, support her and forgive her easy cruelty toward you. For the entire, endless wedding night, you'll be her confidante, her fount and secret link with the invisible. Her advocate and tender mistress. Her soul set free. Her body that one day will radiate pleasure.

Women are cruel. I know only too well. They never liked me. I helped them so many times. They always turned their backs on me, ignored and insulted me.

It doesn't matter. That's how it is. But you shall be free. You'll be above them. You'll be like me. Me. The *introductrice*. Damned, and so very much in demand.

Men can never get hard on that night. Don't worry, whatever you do. I'll give you a simple and effective technique to help them become more erect than they need to be to fulfill your mission. If sexual words aren't enough, and your eyes and buttocks have no effect, then, brave girl, without asking, put your finger in the groom's asshole.

You'll see, he won't be surprised.

Men love it. Love to be treated in a different way. Love for the tables to turn without warning. They like the asshole, their own, others people's. They're used to talking to other men's asses, and those of little boys . . .

Don't be afraid. Push your finger in deep. The man will get hard right away. Gently pull your finger out and play with the rim for a minute or so. I warn you, no more than a minute. Some get so much pleasure from this little game that they faint dead away. Avoid that. If you see the man is passing out, slap him on both cheeks and remind him of his duty. "Sidi, it's your turn, the path is this way, the perfumed garden is ready and waiting."

You must find me coarse. But I'm just telling you the way things are. I don't want to waste time, I have none left. I'm not making light. I don't have the strength. But I do want to define the world for you, sketch its outlines, its boundaries.

A man doesn't know his own cock, that extra limb that bewilders him, makes him burn and makes him yearn.

The cock is a separate being. You have to strike up a conversation with it, and secretly exclude the man. For every cock you have to invent a new language, gestures, murmurs and gazes; ways to approach and win it over, seize and take it to the end of the night and the peak of its pleasures. Very often, the groom will be afraid too. Don't forget to be tender. Look at him tenderly, but don't be sentimental. He'll be moved, grateful. He'll let you take him, tame him, make him bigger, feed him, have him taste saliva, salt, sugar, honey, forest, blood. His own milk.

I'M GOING. SLIMA. I'm leaving, I'm dying.

But the future arrives quickly. It's a happy idea, the future. Optimistic. Infinite.

You'll be there, in that blank time. You're there. Whatever happens through me, you'll be the one who sees up ahead. The lookout.

A being apart. More than now. More than others.

You will not speak. I know.

Only the night will give you that power, that openness. That miracle.

Use it for the good of others. Especially women. All they'll have is you.

In guiding, in dominating the man's cock, you'll be serving your own sex. You'll have needs. You'll know how to satisfy them. You'll be bad in the eyes of others. And so deeply fulfilled. A sun. A moon. A star. The star.

I wish it with all my heart.

Life is treacherous, I know. There's no God here, we both know it.

Only she, She is real. The tall woman. The Berber. The warrior woman who fought the Arabs centuries ago, when they began to invade us and forced us to change. She was courage and cunning. Stubbornness. Freedom. Pride. Our goddess.

Our true queen. Our Cleopatra. Our example. Do you know her? You know who she is, don't you? No? No?

You need to know. Ask around.

Use her as inspiration—her actions and her loyalty to herself, her body, her instincts. Her sex.

Her name is . . . Her name . . . I'm thirsty . . . Slima . . . I'm thirsty . . .

Take my hand, Slima.

I'm thirsty . . . I'm thirsty . . .

Touch my feet. Squeeze them. Squeeze them.

Water, now.

No, my time's run out.

I'm trembling.

It's here. It's come.

Coiling itself around and around me. Big. Long. Climbing. Squeezing.

Look into my eyes. I don't want to go alone.

Look at me.

I'm afraid. I'm afraid.

It's squeezing hard. Hard. HARD.

I'm leaving.

I'm leaving.

Kahina.

The Berber goddess. Her name is Kahina. KA-HI-NA.

Don't betray us, my daughter.

Be worthy.

Let go of my hand.

Let go Slima. Let go.

3

A MAN IS CUTTING A TREE. He's striking the final blows, three, two, one. He stops. Steps away. The tree is big, very big. You see it. You couldn't before, it was out of the camera's field. You can see it now, this falling tree that will fall completely. But first it has to detach from itself, from the rest of its body, its roots deep, deep in the ground. It does. The tree decides to do it. To fall. It's no longer standing. The long body with its roots in the sky, hurls itself and falls little by little, in slow motion, then very, very quickly. Separation occurs. Detachment. One body with two roots. An old body from long ago, which would have lived a long time more, hundreds of years, more than any man. An eternal body is dying, cut in two, divided, no longer in or of the earth. The tree collapses. The speed of the fall, at the very end, accelerates. It is violent, breathtaking. It doesn't look like anything human, it is a speed outside of us in a reality unknown to us, black and strange.

The tree is in pain. I ache for it. For its branches. Each time.

I'm in front of the television set. I devour the images from the movie. My mother Slima is working. I hear her in the next room.

I don't know the name of the tree that just fell. What kind it is.

It's alone now. You know that by sight.

Our tree is lying down, it is dying. Around it are other trees. They look like our tree. Not exactly, to tell the truth. They all have the same mother, probably. Not the same father. Anyway, fathers don't count. Are they brothers? All brothers? Sisters? All sisters? Nephews? Nieces? We don't know. But we see that all the trees on the screen are the same age as our tree on the ground, they have the same green in their branches, the same ocher color down the sides of the body. It's obvious. It's meant to be obvious, the separation and the resemblance. A tree was just cut from the earth. And sky. Its fall has caused a tremor of signs and stars. It is invisible. We imagine it. And it is very real.

We're not going to mourn this tree?

Why not?

What is the point of this murder? And what will become of its roots in the earth? Will they give life to another tree? Will they dare to betray our tree, its body still warm, not completely dead?

And the man, cruel man, what is he doing?

He saw the same thing as us, as me. He didn't miss a moment of this scene, this degradation. He relished the tragic spectacle of his own cruelty. An ax in his hand, he recorded it all. He remained calm. Neutral. He said nothing, expressed nothing.

The man is tall.

He's wearing jeans, a shirt, a belt, cowboy boots.

He's a cowboy.

We're sad.

He's not sad.

It's strange, he's moving away. He doesn't look at the tree. He doesn't touch it. He leaves, just like that. He straightens up, keeps hold of the ax. And he leaves the frame.

It's cruel.

It's frightening.

We don't understand the man. We judge him. I judge him. Mercilessly.

He's a cold man. For the moment, let's not make excuses for him.

He leaves the scene.

We're with the tree. We're on the ground with it. We look at it and don't know what to do. The other trees turn away. They're afraid to look. You can understand why. Death is hard to look at. We close our eyes. We see the trees all slowly closing their eyes. But we're fascinated, enthralled, and we keep looking. Looking without knowing when we too should close our eyes.

Sadness rules the world. The set. And yet the colors are warm, brilliant, violently alive. They always will be. Call it a scandal all you like, these colors won't change, won't vary. We know they are beautiful, a celebration of life. We know. We understand and we are sad. God hears us and joins us in our infinite sadness for this tree cut down, ripped out, its feet severed. God has mercy on us and the tree.

The next three scenes show the beauty of the world's grief for the tree that just departed. Forest. River. Mountain. Grandiose Space. Earth and Sky, united and singing.

There are no men, there is only the world. Only sounds. Another language that we don't understand.

It lasts maybe a minute, the funeral. The world without the tree.

And the man reappears in the middle of it all. He's short and rides a beautiful horse. They both go. They go. They don't explain anything for now. Will God punish the man? Judge him for this crime, for the sadness he's caused? Punish him and throw him in hell for the soul he took in cold blood? Or at least ask him to justify what he did? For our sake, ask him why?

The man and the horse ride away, dissolve into Nature. The credits roll.

My mother's alone in the next room now, resting between two tricks. I'm watching this movie for the tenth time. The credits scroll over music and a song. I don't understand English, but I know almost all the words to the song, *River of No Return.*

The whole movie is in French. Other voices take possession of the actors' bodies, the characters' bodies. It took a while to understand this. One of my mother Slima's customers helped me. He gave me two tapes of the same movie, one in French and the other the original, in English. And he explained the title. *River of No Return.*

Later, just before this customer left for the war, after he'd started calling me "son," we studied all the words of the song together.

Here it is:

> *Ummmhhhhh*
> *If you listen, you can hear it call*
> *Wail-a-ree*
> *Wail-a-ree*
> *There's a river called the River of No Return*
> *Sometimes it's peaceful and sometimes wild and free*
> *Love is a traveler on the River of No Return*
> *Swept on forever to be lost in the stormy sea*
>
>
> *Wail-a-ree*
> *I can hear the river call*

No return, no return
Wail-a-ree
I can hear my lover call: Come to me
No return, no return
I lost my love on the river and forever my heart will yearn
Gone, gone forever down the River of No Return
Wail-a-ree
Wail-a-ree
Wail-a-ree
He'll never return to me
No return, no return
Never

My mother's customer really understood those lyrics, those words. I felt them inside, I grasped them in my own way. With my heart. They spoke of love, of course. Lost love. My mother's man didn't need to tell me that. Sad love on a river without end.

One early morning, he told me he was leaving. My mother wasn't awake yet.

"I'm going tomorrow. I want you to sing this song for me tonight. You have all day to memorize the words. You can read, of course. Right? You're twelve. You go to school. Don't you? Will you do it? I'll do the chorus. I'll do the *Wail-a-ree*. Okay? What do you say? Give me this little gift . . ."

How could I refuse?

He was the most handsome of the soldiers who came to our house to sleep with my mother for a while. To play with me. Talk with me.

He was handsome like an imaginary father. He didn't exist. My mother's job had made him exist. The dream, the impossible fantasy had become reality. Twice a week, this soldier was our father in our new house.

My mother Slima had finally listened to me.

We'd left the terrible neighborhood of Hay al-Inbiâth. As I'd wanted, we moved to the neighborhood of Hay Salam. For as long as possible, we pretended to be just like everyone else. The neighbors finally realized, of course. After only a month. It didn't take long for frustrated men, married or single, to learn the way to our house and my mother's naked body.

I never slept when they were there. I was in the other room. I listened so as not to feel ashamed or overwhelmed by panic.

I know everything. Everything. Everything about sex.

Nothing embarrasses me. It's only sex. Everyone needs it. My mother provides it. Sometimes free. She gives herself to others. And we eat. You have to eat.

WE'VE BEEN IN HAY SALAM for two years. I don't go to the hammam now. I don't like hammams anymore.

I'm watching the movie again. *River of No Return*. I have to memorize the words of the song. Make sure I have them down perfectly inside me.

I thought I knew the movie, every detail, every color. I was wrong. The movie begins with a tree that is killed. That means something. It must mean something. But what?

Now all I can see is this tree that falls.

River of No Return is the story of a tree.

Why sacrifice a tree?

I watch the movie again. I sing along. I understand and don't understand. Suddenly there's another story, another key.

I turn the key.

The tree is dead, its soul rising.

People mourn it.

I mourn it.

We say a prayer together. *River of No Return.*

The words enter me in a different way tonight. A powerful deadly way. I want to reach my hand out. I do. I hold my breath. I leave my soul. I unite with the soul of the tree. We're friends. Our souls run ahead of us. They look at me, urging me on. My body stays with the tree.

I'm in heaven. I learn the song again.

My mother closes the door of her room. A new customer. Another soldier, no doubt.

I close my eyes. My soul no longer belongs to me. The movie keeps playing on our television set. I see it. I listen to it. I stop it. I focus on the first moment.

They cut. They kill. They fell and do not bury. The earth will eventually cover everything.

The song. Again. It returns to my troubled mind. Comes before my blind eyes.

I accompany it. I say the words that carry me along, without fully understanding.

I sing like the song. In rhythm with the song. In another language.

I sing with my man's voice.

I sing and repeat.

First there are voices of women, of angels, who softly sing "woooohh." Men's voices join in. They say, "*No return, no return, no return.*" Then the lone voice of a man takes over, takes control of the song. The credits are on but the song began well before them, just as the soul left the tree.

The singer sings. The chorus backs him up. And I imitate him. I whisper his English words. I say them just after he does.

I invented it all. I think I was singing the first time I wrote something. Awake and unconscious at once, somehow, inspired, possessed by a passing *jinn*. I wrote a strange poem that I've since lost. Forgotten. But I can still taste that inspiration, that unexpected meeting.

I'll have to write again one day. Before I die for good. With that same taste. The trace it left. Searching for heaven in another way. With English words. English, in appearance. Deep inside me, words will always be Arabic. That's the language inside me, there long before me. It sticks to my skin, goes far beyond me, speaks to me in spite of myself. Records our destiny, our days, our nights, my mother's stifled cries, her solitude, her distress, and sometimes her happiness.

I continued learning the song, bringing it gently into myself. My mother's soldier had challenged me. He wanted proof, he believed in me. I had to be a man. Like him, a man. Little soldier. Big soldier.

NOT FAR FROM THE NEIGHBORHOOD of Hay Salam, there was a huge military base. A vast and terrifying wasteland lay between us. I never dared to cross it. It was a land of bandits, real ones, of drunkards cast out by everyone, killers, and drug addicts. A lawless zone next to the largest military base in Morocco. I never understood how that was possible. I once asked our soldier. He didn't have an answer. He simply said:

"That's Morocco!"

That's Morocco?

Another enigma.

After work, the soldier passed through this zone to get to Hay Salam, where he lived, like us. He was never afraid. Probably his military dress and his mother's prayers protected him.

Hay Salam belonged to him.

It was the mid-eighties.

Morocco suddenly needed more soldiers. They were trained in Salé, Kenitra, Meknes, and then sent south, into the Sahara, to defend a desert that had suddenly become a national territory, a sacred cause. A taboo. A mystery. A piece of fiction. Science fiction.

Our soldier was about to finish his two years of training.

He had first arrived when I was eleven. That day I was almost thirteen.

I got used to him very quickly. The room he rented at the home of a Berber from the Sous was not far from our house. He came to see my mother at least twice a week. And I went to see him in his messy bachelor's room four to five times a week. He never complained about my too-invasive presence, my too-naive songs, and my too-skinny butt. To make him love me a little more, I invented a role for myself. Maid. I tidied the mess in his room. Did his laundry. Washed his dishes. The odor of musk in the air at his place was mine. Musk was a link between our two rooms. Our two lives.

Two years of coming and going.

Two years of knowing a man inside and out; a human being, a male sex.

Two years of knowing all there was to know about his words and silences. His quickening breath, his heart going wild from pleasure. His moan, his body's violent fall from heaven.

Two years of being inspired by a man. Copying him, walking like him, standing and falling like him. Inventing a place in the world near his, a parallel path.

Two years.

I saw nothing but him. Him, and my mother Slima. Him, my mother, and the movie, *River of No Return*.

Two years that were ending that evening.

He was being sent to fight in the south for Moroccan honor, Moroccan pride.

He was so dignified next to me, to us.

Now he was going to enter more deeply into the submission forced upon all of us, all Moroccans.

"The Polisario. That's the name of our enemy. They want to steal our Western Sahara."

The soldier said this and laughed.

Later, years later, I understood the meaning of that laugh, its irony and transgression. Its sadness.

I had nothing against the Polisario. I didn't know the Moroccan Sahara.

I knew the soldier.

He was leaving that night.

He was marching toward death.

He knew it.

I knew it.

No one could force this fate to change. Divert, cancel, fight it or get around it.

The Sahara was Moroccan, King Hassan II had decided. In 1975, after the Spanish left, he organized a big march to recover it, make it Moroccan. The Green March.

The soldier had packed his suitcase. I helped. He really wanted me to.

The soldier was going to cry.

My mother didn't care. For her, he was just another customer among so many others.

I had learned the song from the movie. There was no way I was going to betray him. Break down in front of him. Joy was what he came to us for. Joy was my last gift to him.

A song. A little dance. A refrain. A language we made our own at last.

Through the long night we were going to rewrite everything. Never to sleep again.

MY NAME IS JALLAL.

As soon as we moved to Hay Salam, my mother Slima bought a television set. Color. Rare at the time, the mid-eighties.

She did her work. Men. More men. White. Sometimes, but rarely, black. She had a lot of success.

After school, in my blue bedroom, I watched television.

In the green bedroom, my mother sweated it out.

I was never bored.

I did the housework and cooked. My mother took care of the rest.

The Hay Salam years were the time when everything was going to be redefined. My role. Hers. What we would do together and separately, communicating through the wall that linked my room to hers.

I never woke my mother when she was sleeping. Her body had another rhythm from mine, other experiences.

I knew everything.

I sometimes asked a question.

"That's the way it is, my son. I was born for this. For living naked and unafraid of being naked for others. I'm not ashamed."

I still didn't understand.

I watched television. That was where I learned to see things more clearly. The connections between people. Evil. Good. Masks. Languages. Illusions.

We couldn't tell anyone we had a color television. Not the

neighbors or the kids at school. Jealousy—again, still, was everywhere. We had to beware of other people, all people. Nakedness does not mean revealing your soul and your secrets to everyone.

"People don't understand the earth. We don't know how to be real anymore. You must never completely open up to others, my son, not even to people who love you. Resist. Resist. Never tell everything about yourself, your story, your heart. Never give yourself completely. Nobody deserves that honor. Do you understand?"

The color television symbolized that attitude, that way of thinking. That strategy. Of hiding the essential. Hiding the truth. Learning to cast spells. Cancelling out the spells of others. Going along in life, permanently on your guard.

Nobody knew. Nobody got it right about me. Except maybe the soldier. He knew about the color television. He knew it had been invented to speak for us, write our stories for us. "It's our memory," he often said. "It's our friend," I replied. "My friend."

Television showed me another way of thinking about the world and myself.

It gave us movies.

Westerns were my favorites by far. All westerns. One especially, *River of No Return*, of course.

Here's how I discovered it.

It was Sunday, my mother's busiest day. From 10:00 a.m. to 7:00 p.m., it was a parade. Men of all ages. Regulars and new arrivals alike knew they had to behave at our house. Mind their manners. Wait their turn in silence. Not smoke. Not ask for tea—we only served coffee. And, most importantly, never cry out when they came.

Mute, the customers sometimes played cards.

"Everyone knows I'm a prostitute but that's no reason to turn my house into a souk. Rules are rules."

That's what she told them again and again, incessantly.

They waited their turn like good schoolboys. The exam looked as if it was going to be tough. And that excited them. Their eyes betrayed their wildest erotic dreams. They were no longer of this world. Their heads were already with my mother, plunged in her generous body.

"The warmth of your thighs melts my worries away."

One of my mother's soldiers returned only for that. To sleep on my mother's thighs. Thirty minutes. No more. Wake up. Repeat the phrase. And leave.

He was the oldest. Forty-five. He always went last.

That Sunday, he told my mother that we absolutely had to watch television around 8:30. His favorite Western was going to be on.

My mother took a quick shower in the Turkish toilets.

Dinner was ready. Bissara (beans) with olive oil and cumin. Without tomatoes.

It was very cold. Winter no longer wanted to leave, to end.

My mother joined me in my little bed.

We were under the same blanket.

In the same heat.

The rain fell. Hard.

On color television, the movie had already started.

A blond woman sang. Danced and sang. Around her, only men, cowboys happy as children.

I didn't know who she was.

But my mother knew her well.

With sincere adoration, she said:

"That's Marilyn! Marilyn Monroe!"

It was as if she had found a lost sister, passionately loved in another life. Here was proof that love was right to exist and impose its divine law upon us. To leave for no reason and return some quiet day, with no particular event.

A love that went beyond my mother, her gender, her sex, her history. Beyond her circumstances and reality. Movies and Marilyn Monroe drew my mother out of her silence, her constant refusal to exist in words that were said and said again.

"That's Marilyn! That's her! That's her!"

I would have liked to agree with her. But I didn't know the American actress. A blond woman. Very blond. On her head—fire.

Later that night, my mother told me what she knew about her. About her loves.

"She died the year I was born. I know from the radio. They said it several times. The year she left. Suicide, they say. But that's a lie. That woman cannot die. Death cannot catch her. Death is afraid of blonds. The fire on their heads scares death away, every kind of death. Marilyn was sad, very sad, deeply sad, it's true. You see it all the time on her, in her gestures, her way of walking, singing. Laughing. Lowering her eyes for a second or two before she finally dares to look up at others, one other. She acts, play-acts joy and happiness. She believes in it. I believe it. Every time she lets herself be taken by the camera she manages to convince me that life is not only life, there's something else. There is the body—hers, mine, yours, the body of the world. There is beauty. There are rules. Marilyn Monroe teaches me to go beyond appearances. She is the entire world, its origins, development, holes, dark matter, sky and volcanoes. She carries all that in herself. And of course it's heavy. Heavy for a child rejected by everyone, from the beginning, from the first day.

Eternally wandering. Sad she was born and sad she will always be. Sad, because she knows everything, knows everything about men and women. With her, men lose their shame. They say dirty words and tell her everything—buried desires, everyday acts of cowardice, the secrets of the parents. She takes it all in. The smiles. The spit. Tears. Arrogance. Doubts. She travels the world for us. I follow her. I follow her right to the end. She's not dead. She's waiting for me in Paradise. She's watching us too, from there. She sees everything. She knows that tonight, this movie she's in is playing at our house. She's not dead. She's with us. Do you understand? She's here. Do you see her? That is Marilyn Monroe. Repeat after me: Marilyn Monroe. Ma-ri-lyn Mon-roe. Marilyn Monroe. I love her. You have to love her. You have to love her, Jallal. You have to."

MY NAME IS JALLAL.

My mother Slima, before nightfall, at the very start of the night initiated me into the mystery of this woman on fire, in flames. An actress. A solitary being. Naked. Between earth and heaven. In transit. A prophetess. A poet. Ignorant. Inspired. A wanton woman surrounded by love. An actress who shows too much of herself and hides the essential, a pure soul, tears without end. She comes from America. But she isn't only American. She speaks English and to my ears, my heart, it's Arabic.

I haven't seen any other movies she's in.

That night, while *River of No Return* was playing on our television, my mother didn't stop crying for a single second.

I understood the identification. It isn't just blood that unites beings to one another. Souls meet, recognize each other and speak, even when gulfs, oceans lie between them.

They overcome these insignificant barriers. They walk on water. Fly up to the sky. Speak with the prophets. Suddenly recite sacred poems without ever having learned them, Sufi poems written centuries and centuries ago. Chant the Koran, the Bible, *The Thousand and One Nights*.

Souls gaze at each other. They are one.

My mother's name, that night, was Marilyn. She was an infidel, like Marilyn. Like her, unhappy. A whore. A servant. A goddess. She hid herself. *River of No Return* revealed my mother to me in a different way. She wasn't only my mother. She wasn't only mine. She was the mother of others too. The mother and twin sister of Marilyn.

Cinema was invented for this. For making us see our mothers in a new light. Keep them forever. Share them with no reserve, no jealousy.

My name is Jallal.

I am the son of Marilyn Monroe.

IN THE END, the soldiers all left.

My soldier will disappear.

He gave me a gift. Two gifts.

An old Sony VHS player.

A movie. A VHS tape. A western. In two versions, original and dubbed in French.

The tree is not dead. I finally understood.

Without the soldier, without my mother, tirelessly, again and again, I watched *River of No Return*, where colors shatter, explode and caress us. A movie devoid of people, devoid of others. A movie that goes back to the very beginning. Where there is no one. Only danger. Only freedom and its dangers. Only temptations and their misunderstandings.

There are three people in that movie.

The man. The woman. And the little boy.

Tonight, the soldier will leave for the obscure war in southern Morocco. There will still be three on our color television.

My mother will be with a customer. The soldier will quickly say goodbye to her. He'll come to see me. And I'll sing.

The movie will start the same way. The tree that is cut down. It falls. It dies. It's on the ground, takes its last breath. Will it resuscitate tonight?

The movie is that uprooted tree, soon transformed.

It took me a while to grasp it, put the signs into the same thought, the same sentence.

I don't understand French.

I watch the movie and reinvent it my own way. Bodies speak better than languages. I've known that forever.

Tree in Arabic is *chajara*, a feminine word.

Tonight, the *chajara* will fall again. Die again and again.

Tonight, with a song, with my raspy young teenage voice, I'll save this *chajara*. She'll change sex, orientation. Identity.

I'll die with her.

We'll fall together.

We'll rise again. Through faith. My faith. My song. And this promise: Marilyn Monroe is waiting for us, she will never betray us.

THIS HAPPENS IN A CAMP. Nobody but cowboys there. All looking for gold. In vain. They rest. They forget. It's nighttime. A man has returned. He just got out of prison. He cut the tree. And did something else we don't know about yet. He found himself a horse. And headed for the camp. Lost men are drunk. They wait. For a discovery. An apparition. An ending. The crowd is getting bigger and bigger. You can see it all over the screen. A wild crowd at breaking point in search of a fleeting moment of tenderness. They drink. And they drink. And they drink. In the middle of these men, a little boy, a little man. Ten years old. Maybe eleven. He's at home in this dangerous crowd on the brink of despair. He serves them. He knows all of them, the men in this crowd. He wanders like they do. He waits like they do. He hasn't begun to drink yet. He isn't innocent anymore. He's seen everything, here in this camp. The thirsty. The deranged. The mad. The saints. The prostitutes. The priests. The songstresses. The warriors. The dead. The survivors. The leaders. A mother. Marilyn Monroe. Fire on her head. She performs on the stage of the cabaret. In a tent.

The man quickly finds the child. He says: "I'm your father. I've come back to take you back. To find you."

The child asks for proof.

The father pulls out a star. The child has the same one on him.

This doesn't last a minute. They didn't even know each other a moment ago. Now they proclaim themselves father and son.

And they go.

They leave the tender and dangerous crowd. The crowd in love with Marilyn Monroe. Kay. Her name in the movie is Kay. She's on stage. She sings. She shows her legs, her shoulders, her arms. Her soul. She radiates gentleness. She isn't vulgar. Her gestures are almost childlike. Her words are prayers. The men have opened their mouths. They no longer care about booze. With Kay, they rise very high. They aren't greedy gold-diggers anymore. They regress. They play like children.

Kay is mother to all.

Father and son have crossed the whole screen, the whole frame. They are now in Kay's dressing room.

The son introduces his new father to the singer.

The father looks at her kindly, with an uneasy respect.

The singer and the son say goodbye to each other. Embrace. It doesn't last long.

That's the end of part one.

These three characters will not see each other again. There is no reason for that to happen.

Now the dream can begin and cinema show its true power. The impossible will become possible.

Outside of the world. Fleeing. On a fragile raft. A family. The son, the father and the singer survive a flood. They are being chased by Indians. Impending death forces them to drift on a raging river. The hope of another paradise compels them to stay together, to save their skin, their souls, their bodies. Try being a family. Reinvent family. Hatred. Betrayal. Love, in the end.

The tree wasn't cut down for nothing. It has come back to life. It was used to build a raft, that simple and strong raft.

River of No Return is also the story of a raft that goes on and on ... The intrepid river doesn't stop it. Death will be its enemy but never break it.

The tree died that first time. At the very beginning.

It rose to heaven.

The movie takes place in another world. A Hereafter where the tree can live again, be transformed.

Resurrection is not a fiction. Cinema proves it. Marilyn Monroe is convinced of it. My mother and I, too.

We weep.

All three of us.

I run to the television and kiss it.

I want the blessing of Marilyn Monroe. I want her fire.

Just at that moment, the soldier returns.

My mother wipes her tears. She stands up. And silently leaves for the room next door.

The soldier says:

"See you in a while, kid. Don't forget me . . ."

I stay glued to the television screen. I enter it.

I join the other family. On the raft.

I sing *River of No Return.*

And I understand that a little bit later, I will sing it just the way it should be sung, like Kay. The soldier will be proud of me.

I know that now.

The eyes and hair of Marilyn Monroe confirm my intuition: life doesn't stop.

Something happens. I see it. I'm there now.

I change realities, really and truly enter fiction, cross the border, take on other colors.

Time stops.

I'm in the true.

In the song.

On a tree.

II. For Love

1

"YOU DON'T LIKE the singer Samira Said? Is that true, Slima? It can't be! Everyone in Cairo loves Samira Said. She's a very big star in the Arab world. She's Egyptian. We really think of her as Egyptian now ... You don't like Samira Said? You're Moroccan and you don't like Samira Said? Have you no shame? I'm sure your son Jallal loves her."

For once, I'd agreed to accompany my mother Slima to her favorite beauty salon.

I was very entertained by the hairdresser's chitchat with his many clients.

I had no opinion of Samira Said, but my mother really didn't like her.

The hairdresser didn't want to believe it. Could not. And set himself a challenge that annoyed my mother no end, to make her change her mind.

"Tell me, Slima ... What Egyptian and Arab singers do you like?"

"Do you know Aziza Jalal?"

"Ah! The other Moroccan singer who's become a star in Egypt! Is that who you like? The one with the big intellectual glasses?"

"Aziza Jalal has more distinction, more class."

"So everyone says. But her angelic voice and perfection leave me cold."

"Her voice is like the divine Ismahane's. You must have noticed."

"Not you too? My dear Slima, you've fallen into the trap of that comparison!"

"It's the truth. She's as great as Ismahane."

"Aziza Jalal and Ismahane are too cold. Too much the diva and high priestess. They overplay the mystery card."

"You're wrong."

"Anyway, I'm right to love Samira Said. She's more deserving. No one gave her anything. No one made things easier for her. She's a fighter. She's the one who's still fighting."

"What do you mean by that?"

"Aziza Jalal retired, didn't she?"

"Yes."

"And why?"

"She didn't want to sing anymore. She had nothing more to give her audience. She was probably too exhausted. So . . . so . . . she retired. I respect that decision."

"No, no, my dear Slima, that's not that the real reason. She stopped singing because her rich Saudi husband asked her to. She was only thirty when she retired. All that to please Hubby. To please a man who believes that a woman's place is in the home. Slima, don't tell me you support that kind of decision, that hypocrisy!"

"I respect . . . yes . . . I understand . . . Aziza."

"Respect isn't the issue, darling. It's comparing two Arab stars from Morocco. Aziza Jalal and Samira Said."

"And?"

"Samira Said is still out there fighting. Taking the hits. Defending herself . . ."

"For who?"

"For you. For women. Strange you haven't noticed! You're smart. What exactly do you have against Samira Said?"

"She's not natural. She lacks sincerity, truth."

"Since when is art about being natural?"

"What do you mean?"

"Songs are mainly inventions, constructions. Natural is boring. Building a persona over many years is what I respect in artists like Samira Said. Strong commitment, all the way. Real conviction that goes beyond singing. Intelligence put toward a real cause. Freedom you can see the moment she appears . . ."

"You're making a good case . . ."

"I love women who don't let themselves be dominated by men. And Samira Said is that kind of woman, besides being a gutsy modern singer . . . So stop giving us the runaround. Tell us the real reason you don't like her . . . What have you got against Samira Said?"

The debate on this frivolous topic was conducted with utter seriousness, with passion. But in truth, the reason people talk about stars is to avoid talking about themselves. That's why stars were invented, according to the hairdresser.

"I really do not like Samira Said. I don't like that singer. Do you understand? I don't like anything Moroccan."

This last sentence, calmly spoken, sent a shock through the entire salon. All the customers had their eyes on my mother.

"Aren't you ashamed?"

The judgment came down in one fell swoop, from all of them at once.

My mother pretended to read her magazine, *Al Mawed*.

"And your son Jallal?" the hairdresser suddenly asked, after a minute of discomfort that seemed endless.

I wanted to answer. My mother beat me to it:

"My son Jallal is like me. He doesn't like Samira Said."

Of course the hairdresser didn't believe her.

"Let him answer. He's old enough, isn't he?"

Again my mother spoke in my stead.

"My son is mine. He likes what I like. He's my memory and my forgetting. He'll like what I tell him to like. He'll be what I tell him to be."

She uttered these last words bluntly. Tonelessly. She was not being light anymore.

After a long moment of silence and discomfort, she spoke again.

"My son will carry me as I carry him. He comes from me. I'm his origins, his country, his future. I've found him again. I've just found him again. We're in Cairo. We'll go to the ends of our fate. Right to the limit. Every day since I've been able to see him and touch him again, I've urged him to shed a skin that's not ours. Morocco? What's Morocco? A country? An idea? A feeling? Why am I forced to keep on wearing it, here in Egypt? I left that country, I left that world behind. I also left that country's language, its Arabic, the way they say words in Arabic there. I broke out of that mold. Three years of silence and darkness helped me to think, change, see things clearly. They wanted to kill me. I'm dead. The woman you all see before you is someone else.

I shed blood. A lot of blood. They took everything from me. I have the right to rebuild. To start from scratch. Now, in 1988. Here, in your country. Do you get me? Do you grant me that right? Cairo doesn't only belong to you Egyptians. The city is mine too. It belongs to all rootless Arabs. I choose it. I'm taking it for my second life. My rebirth. I just arrived. It was one . . . one year ago . . . One year already! I'm one year old. My son is barely three months old.

I'm not Moroccan. My son isn't either. End of story. Don't talk to me about that past, please."

"And Samira Said? Morocco's against her too, you know. There's a rumor going around . . ."

The hairdresser was no longer out to attack and provoke.

My mother's rather complicated, abstract speech had baffled and intrigued him. He wanted to understand, to know what had happened. But he was going about it the wrong way.

My mother asked:

"What rumor?"

"About the porn. Samira Said made a porn movie, so they say. To get ahead. They say she slept with a lot of sheikhs in the Gulf countries to become a star in Egypt and the Arab world. Supposedly they're the ones who backed her and are backing her still. But, something about the story escapes me. She's very intelligent. I don't see her making porn. Sure, people will do anything to succeed, but she's really smart, not like other singers. There's something about the story that I don't get . . ."

The hairdresser was passionate about this piece of gossip. He wanted to keep feeding us details but my mother didn't let him.

"And where did this rumor start? Do you know? Morocco, I suppose. She couldn't have been born anywhere else. No other country pushes its citizens to the brink the way Morocco does. Tries to destroy them at all costs. Follows them everywhere with its curse. I don't know if Samira Said slept with those petrodollars, but in any case she was right to go, leave Morocco, get the hell out. You can't succeed in Morocco. People will do anything to stop you, control you, keep you down. They force you to whore yourself. They take your money then pretend they don't know you. They call you a slut, a disgrace, an infidel. But they're the infidels. Totally heartless. I'm sure Samira Said didn't make that porn movie. Now that they have no hold over her, the Moroccans are furious and invented the story. They don't understand why we'd go anywhere else and flourish. It's beyond their understanding. Right away, you're a traitor. She was right to leave and defy them all. To go far away. If they think success means becoming a whore, then all Moroccan women are whores. Aren't they?"

The Egyptian women waiting their turn listened open-mouthed to my mother's
politics.

The hairdresser couldn't believe it. He felt he'd almost accomplished his mission. With a touch of irony, he complimented my mother. He said she had a bit of an intellectual look.

"You've got to be kidding, darling! Me, an intellectual?! A whore, yes! Officially a whore. An intellectual, never! I leave books and ideas to others, those other people who must despise us even more than the rich. A whore, yes, I've never denied it. A scholar, not on your life!"

My mother's frankness disturbed the room. One woman rose and, shooting her a long severe look, left the salon grumbling.

"Oh! I'm sorry, ladies, I speak too freely. Are Moroccans too free for you? Am I offending you? You've never heard anyone talk like me? Should a woman keep her mouth permanently shut? Even in Cairo?"

The hairdresser didn't give them time to answer. He suggested something else, a moment's relaxation.

"Why don't we play a song by Samira Said? Like her hit from '85, 'I'll never give you up.' What do you think? Is that alright, my darlings? Is that okay? No one will be upset? And after that, we'll talk. We'll see if this revolutionary Moroccan

will finally let her heart be touched by her compatriot ...
Okay? Okay? They say that music soothes the soul. Don't
they? All right then, let's listen to Samira Said ..."

The other women smiled kindly.

My mother lowered her eyes.

The hairdresser pressed Play.

Those who hadn't heard the singer before expected something light and forgettable. But the song was anything but
trivial. War was declared from the very first note. This woman,
Samira Said, was not afraid of repeating herself, of saying the
same words over and over, fighting a solitary battle. The battle
of love, of course.

> *You whose love gave my life flavor, color*
> *I'll never give you up, whatever happens*
> *Whatever happens*
> *And if a word was said in anger*
> *And injured our hearts*
> *We forget our sadness*
> *And which of us spoke,*
> *It's through the soul that we love*
> *We'll always be together*
> *All our lives, together*
> *Whatever happens*
> *I loved you*
> *When I found you*
> *Before my eyes a distant dream*
> *Was in my eyes*
> *Out of reach*
> *The next moment it was in my hand*
> *Who chooses to leave paradise?*
> *Why destroy our own hopes*

And spend the rest of our lives regretting
What happened?
You whose love gave my life flavor, color
I'll never give you up, whatever happens
Whatever happens
Never
Never
Give you up
Whatever happens.

IT TOOK OUR BREATH AWAY.

The song lasted almost seven minutes. It was so powerful. And the voice of Samira Said rang out from the heart of the war. War to the bitter end, the final breath.

She sang with her voice and her body, her words like shots from a cannon. She reinvented Arabic, the way of saying, of singing, Arabic and Egyptian words. It seemed impossible to doubt her sincerity. Impossible to imagine turning our backs on the battle this woman continued to tirelessly fight. Her love was for a man. We were sure about that, at first. Then as she charged and charged again, the more she repeated the words, the less sure we became. Love, the great and sublime love she wielded with incredible power, could not only be for a man, inspired by a man. This battle went beyond the man and beyond all men.

After the song, my mother said, as if reading my thoughts:

"The man she's talking about in that song doesn't exist. No man can be so worthy of such love and sacrifice."

The others in the room did not understand.

The hairdresser, ever provocative, looked at my mother, took her hair in his hands and whispered in her ear:

"So you still don't like Samira Said?"

My mother turned to me. Smiled at me without really smiling.

"I want to be blond. Dye my hair blond. Right now. Do that for me, please ..."

What had happened to her? What did this have to do with Samira Said, who was a true brunette?

The hairdresser, taken aback, ventured a piece of advice:

"Come on, now ... darling ... It's the end of the '80s! Blonds are out. Blond is tacky ... Stay on the side of strength, stay with black, like Samira Said. You have no right to betray her. To drop her again ..."

My mother looked at me once more. In her eyes I read the words she was about to say. She may have changed her mind about Samira Said but deep inside, her first and essential loyalty was to one particular woman. The woman, the sister for all time, whom she had introduced me to and made me love in Morocco, in Salé, in a movie. Our movie. *River of No Return.* A blond orphan actress.

"I want to be blond, my friend. Right now. That's an order. Blond. Do you understand? Blond like ... like ... like ..."

She hesitated two or three seconds. Everyone in the salon was waiting with bated breath to hear what she was going to say.

Blond like who?

"Blond like Marilyn Monroe. Exactly like Marilyn Monroe."

Nobody dared challenge her choice.

Marilyn Monroe also had a special, sacred place on this side of the Arab world. Cairo, our capital of film production, had its own mythical stars, but like all of us, the city retained a fond, pious, and sincere memory of the American blond.

2

EVEN WHEN THE MUEZZIN made the call to prayer they didn't stop. They continued to torture me, to rape me.

I was on the other side of the river Bouregreg, in Rabat. I saw our bank, our city, Salé. I saw the water tower at the entrance to the Bettana district. And beyond Bettana our neighborhood Hay Salam.

It wasn't a dream, Jallal. It was a nightmare. True. Real. Endless.

I thought I was going to die. I was sure of it. So I thought tenderly of you, my Jallal. And of our soldier who'd just gone to war in southern Morocco.

Muslims do not exist.

There are no more Muslims, my son.

Do you understand? It's over. Going back is out of the question. Leave Cairo? Go back to Morocco? Never! With everything they did to me, the hatred they unleashed ... No matter how I cried out, screamed, their hearts never softened. I was the cow on the ground. There were more and more knives. All men! All men, of course! They said that since I was a whore and did nothing to hide it, they had to treat me like a whore. Honor me that way. Rape me from morning to night. In the middle of the night. At every moment.

But they didn't start with rape right away. They were even quite pleasant at first, courteous. Falsely sweet. Well mannered. Well dressed. We were in a real office. Through the windows I saw the sky and Rabat's famous landmark, the Hassan Tower, where Mohammed V, the father of King Hassan II is buried. Do you know it? Do you remember? I could hear the everyday lives of other people going on downstairs. I heard a lady yelling at her little housemaid from time to time. And I heard the elevator going endlessly up and down.

Several times I was offered mint tea, gazelle horns, and a delicious *mille-feuille*. It was the best *mille-feuille* I'd had in my entire life. I said so to one of the three men interrogating me. I will never forget his reply:

"It is the special *mille-feuille* of the royal palace."

I was very frightened then. Cold fear bolted through my entire body.

I finally grasped what awaited me. And suddenly I remembered the horrible, terrifying stories that my soldiers in Hay Salam sometimes told.

I didn't finish the *mille-feuille*. It didn't taste the same.

It disgusted me to be put on the same footing as the people at the royal palace.

The three men saw my disgust.

Then the tone changed. In the blink of an eye.

"You know where you are, don't you? You know who we are. Don't you?"

I thought very hard of you, my son, my little Jallal. And I said goodbye to you. I didn't want to associate you with the hell that was flinging its doors open before me.

Goodbye, my son. Goodbye, my darling. I regret bringing you into the world. I regret it. Believe me, I regret it. Now you're going to be alone, wander alone, and no one will give you anything to eat. Goodbye, my soul, my accomplice, my protector, my little brother. Goodbye for now. Go. Go. Go, far away from here. Run. Flee. Flee them all. We'll be reunited one of these days. Everyone. I'll find my mother Saâdia, who adopted me, and you. One day. In another world. Goodbye, for now. Goodbye, Jallal. Goodbye, Jallal.

"You're not saying anything … Look up … Yes, like that, good … Like that … I'm Melloul. He's Hammadi. And the other guy's Sabti. And you? Is Slima your real name?"

My memory went blank.

I said nothing for a moment.

I wasn't a prostitute anymore. I wasn't being a prostitute anymore. I had to invent another character. And most of all, I had to bury in some obscure well the rare secrets the soldier confided in Hay Salam before going to war in southern Morocco. Forget them.

They were smarter than me, those three men. They read my mind.

"Your soldier's dead. They threw his body in the sea. Why was he against the Moroccan Sahara? He worked for the Polisario. You knew that, didn't you? You know. We know that you know."

Holding out against sex-starved men is my job. Giving them only what I want to give. Very little.

But how to hold out against the secret police?

I might as well tell you right now, my son, I couldn't do it. I couldn't.

These weren't men. They were butchers. Monsters.

They weren't sex-starved like other men. They were only interested in blood, inflamed by blood that flowed a long time.

I lowered my head. Once again I became the little girl lost in the saint's mausoleum in Rhamna. Before my mother Saâdia adopted me.

They removed their jackets. Rolled up their shirtsleeves.

They approached. Standing in a circle around me.

I was sitting in the middle of the room. On a chair. I still had a glass of mint tea in my hand.

One of the three men reached out, took my glass, finished what little tea remained, and set it on the floor.

Then the war began for real.

"What was your soldier's name?"

He had no first name, our soldier. Did he, my son? Or last name either. He was a soldier. The soldier.

A lot of soldiers came to our house. I remember the names of every one of them. His we never felt the need to know. He was a soldier, and that was that.

I don't know his name. I never knew it.

They didn't believe me.

They asked the same question ten, twenty times. I said the same thing each time.

That's when I received my first slap.

He walked toward me. He repeated what the other one had said, the one who's name was Hammadi. And he slapped me.

I fell off my chair. My head smashed against the floor. I was stunned. I didn't pass out.

They came closer, all three. And let their eyes talk.

And in their eyes I saw all that awaited me. Hell. Refined tortures.

What was I going to do? What could I do?

Betray the soldier?

No. Never.

You'd have done the same, Jallal. We owe him so much! He was the most beautiful surprise we'd ever had. He was our family. Your father. Your big brother. My friend. My husband. He protected us. Fed us. He brought us fruit, pictures, tenderness.

Do you remember all that, my Jallal?

Is he still there inside you, the white soldier, the *fassi*?

Don't forget him. Don't commit that crime. Don't go near that kind of betrayal.

"He went to war. In the south. The Sahara. To fight the Polisario. That's all I know."

Still lying on the ground, I dared to make this reply, this revelation that revealed nothing.

They were not pleased. Not at all.

"Are you making fun of us, bitch? Do you really think we don't know? We know everything. Everything! But we want a confession. Confess while there's still time. For now, you're in an office in the center of Rabat. Who knows where you'll be tonight? Confess! Tell us all you know about the soldier . . . His family in Fez . . . His friends in Fez . . . His strategies . . . His opinions . . . and why he decided to join the conspiracy . . ."

The one called Hammadi crouched down and shouted his dangerous sentences in my ears. While saying the word "conspiracy," he seized the lobe of my left ear and pinched it extremely hard.

I screamed like the damned.

"That's only the beginning, wretch. Confess . . . Confess . . ."

I ventured:

"What conspiracy, sir? Against who?"

His response was scathing. Terrifying. He shouted.

"Stop messing with us! Against King Hassan II . . . Morocco . . . all of us . . . Is the return of anarchy what you want? Talk . . .! Tell us everything, go on . . . The soldier and his friends . . ."

Now the other two were bending over me. I smelled their breath—identical. The breath of heavy smokers, *Favorites* brand.

As I said nothing, one grabbed my hair and pulled it violently.

I didn't cry out.

"I'm just a prostitute. The soldier was one of my few clients. He came from Fez. He was handsome. Very handsome. He didn't need to pay me. He could come whenever he wanted. My door was always open to him. In a way, he was part of . . ."

A poisonous slap struck my cheek. I didn't know which of them gave it to me.

"Your love affair with the soldier? Keep it to yourself! Get it, bitch!?"

Got it. Yes, got it.

"What did he talk to your son about? How he hated the king? Hated the Moroccan Sahara?"

That's when I stopped talking for good.

I knew things, of course. I'd heard things, of course.

For them, Morocco was a sacred fiction. For me, the soldier was home. Yours and mine.

"Let's get down to business. We have no choice. Don't you agree, my friends? We'll do *Lawrence of Arabia* on her. What do you say? It's a good start . . . Don't you think?"

At the time I didn't know what *Lawrence of Arabia* was.

Now I know. I don't need to watch that movie again.

They stood me up. One of them ripped off my long nightgown. All I had on then was my underwear.

One took my left breast, the other my right.

The third stepped back.

"Go on . . ."

They started to fondle my breasts. Slowly.

"Is that good? Do you like that?"

They seized my nipples and pinched, gently at first and then suddenly with violence. Long and very hard.

I passed out, I think.

They revived me.

A lounge chair awaited me. They laid me on it face down.

The first took my wrists and pulled my arms hard.

The second sat on my calves to keep me still.

The third, the boss, was holding a long thin bamboo cane.

"Pull hard on her wrists! I want her to cry tears of blood . . . And you, keep holding her down, don't let her move . . . Come on guys, get to work . . ."

That torture seemed simple, not really dangerous. But it was the worst.

At each blow of the bamboo stick, my soul left my body for a second and then returned.

I raised my head. The first man smiled kindly.

I turned to look behind me. The second did the same.

Using my body, they reenacted a scene from *Lawrence of Arabia.*

They were enjoying themselves. They egged each other on.

The chief was satisfied.

"Perfect, my friends. That time, everyone got right into character, including our pretty whore . . . Get ready . . . Scene I, take two . . . Action!"

Right then, I would have liked to be able to die, depart, travel in the afterlife. I would have liked to be able to scream for relief.

Instead, I wept. Tears of blood. As the leader had commanded.

At the end of this torture session, they pulled off my underwear and inserted the bamboo between . . .

I wasn't feeling anything by then. My flesh was dead.

But I wasn't.

"You're going to talk, bitch! You're going to talk, slut! No one betrays Morocco and gets away with it. You're going to tell us everything. The soldiers. The officers. The noncommissioned officers. And you're going to tell us about the general. Dlimi. We know he came to see you too."

They had written their own fiction. And they wanted me to enter it, in spite of myself.

"General Dlimi actually did come to see me once. As a customer. Nothing more."

They didn't believe me, of course.

Then they asked about the general's sexual preferences.

I said that I never betray my customers' secrets.

"The bitch is honest. She's playing it honest . . . So whores are honest now? Since when?"

Forever, I answered deep inside. And tried to find something interesting to reveal about him.

"He likes sodomy."

"So what else is new? All Moroccans like sodomy . . ."

"You too?"

They looked at each other. Burst out laughing. Laughed a long time.

"We'll give her *Lawrence of Arabia 2*. What do you say?"

The leader, Sabti, sat on my naked buttocks.

Hammadi stood on the right side of my body, Melloul on the left. Each took one of my arms and pulled it as far as it would go.

And the leader opened his fly.

A part of me exploded then. Was pulverized. Annihilated. Forever.

The pain was beyond anything I could imagine.

Nothing remained of my body but atrocious suffering.

They dismembered me.

Beat me.

Spit on me.

Raped me.

All at the same time.

I did not cry out. I had no more strength. I opened my mouth wide. No sound came out. No life. Only the desire to die. And a pure thought, a final prayer for you, my son.

The name that came to my mind just before I passed out, was horrifying: El-Hadj Kaddour El Yousfi.

The most notorious official torturer in the Kingdom of Morocco.

I was so frightened by the famed and terrible name of that man—butcher—executioner—that I ended up going some other place for good.

When I woke up, the famous torturer wasn't there, beside or in front of me.

I didn't know where I was. I'll never know.

DARKNESS EVERYWHERE. Everywhere.

Darkness and nakedness. My naked body.

Darkness, nakedness, and animal noises coming from the ceiling and clamoring on and in my head.

Calm as an abandoned hammam and then, every five minutes, a storm of hellish noises, bleating, bellowing, barking, cries of every kind.

Animals on the verge of slaughter uttering desperate appeals in one last breath, one last hope, touching, hideous, haunting.

After a few days, I realized that it was a recording, activated automatically every fifteen minutes. Night and day.

I thought I'd never get used to it, the racket, the war on the ceiling and in my head.

How long did I go without sleeping? A month? Two months?

Perhaps eternity.

I thought I wouldn't survive those apocalyptic noises. And yet, in my total collapse, my decline, my slow death, a miracle occurred. Having failed to kill me, the noises finally became my companions. My bearings. My friends. I grew to recognize them one by one, those make-believe animals, those voices in the throes of death. I called out to them sometimes. Little by little, I went mad with them, with and because of them.

I talked.

It was those voices that enabled me to speak. Encouraged me to speak.

Speak. Speak. Speak. At last.

You knew me in silence, Jallal. In action without words.

There, far away, between two worlds, near the torturer El-Hadj Kaddour El Yousfi, I shouted words. I murmured, whispered, caressed words.

I was talking to the animals.

The animals talked to me.

Do you believe me, my son? Do you believe me, little Jallal? I could do nothing else. I'm illiterate. Uneducated.

I communicated with animals that did not exist. They killed and released me. Thanks to the animals, I was able to withstand the torture in the end.

The Sahara. The Polisario. General Dlimi who wanted to assassinate King Hassan II. The soldier-conspirators who came to visit. Political discussions. I ended up confessing everything, as you can easily guess.

But him I protected. I swear to you. I swear. Don't be angry with me, my son. I said nothing about your soldier. Not about him or his soul, or the sanctity of his time in our home. Nothing. Nothing.

I exaggerated my revelations about the others in order to protect him. Dead at the bottom of the ocean where they threw him, I still hid him. I kept him alive.

He was alive. He was alive.

Alive where?

I don't know. But he was alive.

The day they let me go, El-Hadj Kaddour El Yousfi said in a paternal voice, strangely gentle:

"My condolences, madam. Your soldier is dead. Died for Morocco, defending the Moroccan Sahara against our enemies, the Polisario and Algeria, which supports them. My condolences."

The day of my release was the day of another death. The confirmation of the soldier's death.

I spat on the legendary torturer.

He did nothing. Maybe he no longer had the strength.

He was probably tired, beyond tired, from all the torture he'd inflicted on so many bodies. Moroccans, young and old, who had an ideal for the country and whom he annihilated.

He stopped History.

He'd killed so many people, taken so many souls. Snuffed out the light in so many eyes. My spit on his face was probably a relief.

"Your soldier died in 1986. Long before your arrest."

Why had they tortured me, then? Who had given the order? The Interior Minister Driss Basri? The king himself?

I spat on him a second time.

He was nothing now, that torturer, that servant more servile than all Moroccans put together.

I stared him down.

His eyes were dead.

"Go, my girl, before it's too late. Leave this country. Leave this Morocco where there's no more room for either you or me. Go. Go . . ."

He shed a tear. With just one eye.

He wept with just one eye. The left.

He wasn't very old. Fifties. He looked twice that.

All the evil and all the horrors he'd committed were coming back to haunt him. Obsess him. Frighten him.

He was paying.

My gobs of spit must have done him some good.

"Go. Leave here. Never come back. Ever. Even your neighbors the Oufkirs ended up leaving, escaped. Leave. Go . . ."

That's how I learned that for the three years I was left to rot in a barbaric hole, General Oufkir's children were in the cell next door. They'd tried twice in the seventies to kill Hassan II.

Do you know the Oufkirs?

No?

It doesn't matter.

When I left my prison, I found myself in a valley. It was spring. There were roses everywhere. Ocher everywhere. I recognized the south of Morocco, though I'd never been there before. I recognized the *ksours*. Almond trees. Palms. That unreal beauty. Paradise. Truly paradise.

I found a *wadi*.

I sat down.

I mourned for the soldier.

I thought about the soldier in another way.

I called up a happy memory. The three of us.

The River of No Return.

A single scene came to mind.

You know it by heart, Jallal. Me too. Him too.

It's at the end of the movie.

Marilyn Monroe, the cowboy and the boy have managed to get across the river. They've been through hell, survived the attacks of Indians and bandits. They're in the city now. Marilyn leaves to go find her husband, who betrayed the cowboy at the beginning of the movie by trying to kill him and steal his horse. She finds him playing poker. He's a pretty boy who doesn't care about her anymore. He's already forgotten her. She warns him the cowboy is looking for him, out for vengeance. The pretty boy goes into the street, toward the cowboy, and points his gun at him. Marilyn tries to stop him. He throws her to the ground. He draws his gun on the cowboy, who has no weapon. He shoots. For a moment, that's what we think. But in fact, it's someone else who has fired, and not at the cowboy but the pretty boy. He falls. Marilyn reappears, rushes to the boy—he has saved his father. The boy is crying, "I had no choice . . . I had no choice . . ." Marilyn takes him in her arms: "It was him or your father . . . You had no choice . . ."

And so the son and his father are reunited, both part of the same drama now. The father had gone to jail because he'd killed a man by shooting him in the back. Throughout the movie, the son criticizes his father for this act of cowardice. The cowboy repeatedly justifies his act. The son doesn't believe him.

The end of the movie reconciles these two hearts in the same tragedy.

To save your life, it may be necessary to kill, at one time or another. Kill another person to survive.

Marilyn takes the little bag she keeps her red high heels in, the shoes she wore onstage at the cabaret. They're all that remains of her past.

She heads for the town saloon.

She returns to her past, to what she does best.

Sitting on a piano, wearing a gold dress that reveals her gorgeous legs, she sings *River of No Return* in a heartrending way. Tragically. Her face is terribly beautiful and her eyes incredibly soft.

She is sexy, sexual, but what she radiates, what is expressed through her is so tender. Beautiful, tender. Childlike, tender.

The customers in the saloon understand. The men and a few rare women draw closer and with understanding in their eyes, support her. Silently, they sing along.

I remembered all that. And I sang too.

At the end the people all applaud with ardor.

Then the cowboy, our cowboy appears. He crosses the doting crowd and reaches Marilyn. They look at each other for a second or two. They know. No need to speak. On the voyage down the infernal river, they began to have feelings for each other. No point in resisting. There is an opportunity to be seized. To try and continue living together as three. And return to the intimacy of the raft.

The cowboy lifts Marilyn off the ground. Throws her over his left shoulder. She pretends to protest. He leaves the saloon, puts her the car next to the boy, and gives her his jacket to cover up with.

She says: "Where are we going?"

He answers: "Home."

I shivered.

A tear rolled down my cheek.

The car starts moving and leaves town. Passing the saloon, Marilyn takes off her shoes, the red heels, and throws them on the ground.

The camera stays on the shoes. I reach out my hand. I take them. I don't have a cowboy. I'll have to return to my old job.

In Marilyn's shoes. Inside her skin. Her struggle. Her sadness. Her tragedy. And in spite of everything, with hope.

The car drives away. A chorus of virile voices can be heard.

They sing *River of No Return* again. It is solemn, a grandiose prayer.

The emotion is still powerful. It will not fade. The journey continues. The tears will never stop.

Marilyn's red shoes fit me well.

I try them on again. And again.

I'm in southern Morocco. I just got out of prison.

I get up.

I walk.

Next to Marilyn.

Like her.

With her voice.

With her white, pale skin.

I run.

She runs with me.

A muezzin suddenly begins the call to prayer. I immediately think of my torturers. The calls to God excited them, almost seemed to encourage them to rape me more violently. Without respite. Without mercy. For no reason. I'd already confessed everything. They kept me for the pleasure of destroying me completely.

It was noon.

The other executioner, El-Hadj Kaddour El Yousfi, must have been doing the same thing at right that moment. To another woman. Or man.

In that place, I understood, my son, and I'll tell you again and again, there are no more Muslims. There are only obedient, heartless slaves, thirsty for power, blood, semen, cries.

I took Marilyn's red shoes. And I left. For Agadir.

I knew I'd find sisters in that tourist town, lost strays like me, sacrificed like me. The living dead. Saints.

I'd find work. My old job.

And get ready to leave. With determination.

As quickly as possible.

Flee to Cairo.

Find you again, my son, my Jallal, in Cairo, where I managed to send you just before they arrested me, with the miraculous help of a wealthy client.

Burn my Moroccan passport.

Burn my Moroccan identity card.

Be born again for you, Jallal. For us.

Cling to that dream. To Marilyn.

3

"CALL ME . . . MOUAD . . ."

"Mouad?!"

"My real name is Jean-Marie . . . But please, call me Mouad."

"Mouad Mouad . . ."

"Do you like the name?"

"It's a name from before . . . before Islam . . ."

"I know."

"Do you know Islam? Are you Muslim?"

"I'm Belgian. From Brussels."

"And . . . what are you doing in Cairo? . . ."

"Mouad . . . call me . . . Mouad."

"Very well. Mouad."

"What about you?"

"Me?"

"What's your name?"

"Slima."

"Pleased to meet you, Slima."

"Pleased to meet you, Mouad! Shall we have a drink?"

"I don't drink."

"You don't drink?"

"No, I don't drink."

"Don't people drink where you come from, in Belgium?"

"Oh yes, people drink a lot in Belgium. Not me."

"You never have?"

"Not for five months."

"Don't you miss it? Wine is good . . ."

"I just got back from Mecca."

"I beg your pardon?"

"I became Muslim . . . A bit Muslim . . ."

"Mecca? Really?"

"I've worked in Saudi Arabia for ten years. I fell in love with the desert of Arabia."

"Like Lawrence of Arabia."

"Yes, like him. Do you know Lawrence of Arabia? Did you learn about him in school?"

". . . Yes, that's right, at school. A very Moroccan school."

"And French?"

"I learned to jabber along with my clients. Mostly foreigners."

"I understand."

"You're my first Belgian."

"I'm honored."

"Do you have any Tylenol? Tylenol from Europe, not the kind they make here, which is useless . . ."

"Yes, I do . . . several boxes, as a matter of fact . . . Do you get headaches often?"

"All the time."

"We'll go to my place . . ."

I MET SLIMA at the Hotel Semiramis.

I'm a chronic insomniac. I'd go to the casino hotel to kill time and keep myself from getting even more depressed.

She was beautiful. But damaged. Small. Very small. Beyond exhausted.

She should have retired long before. She probably couldn't afford to.

I entered the casino, filled with wealthy Gulf Arabs and prostitutes, all Moroccan and heavily made-up.

She was in the middle of a group of women you couldn't miss. They all laughed in a provocative, sensual, exciting and vulgar way. They all smoked. Except her. Men from the Gulf countries hovered around her. It was two in the morning. But in Cairo, the night was just beginning.

The Moroccan women were professional. They knew what they were doing. The men at the casino had eyes only for them.

Like me.

I'd had a taste for Moroccan women for over twenty years.

I lived and worked in Jeddah, Saudi Arabia. And I came to spend my weekends in Cairo as often as I could.

For the Moroccan women.

I really liked them. Sincerely. I couldn't explain that mystery, my extraordinary attraction to them, how good I felt when I was with them, in their arms. Some of them thought I was crazy. This desire for Moroccan women was crazy, yes. And I loved being lost with them, naked in a different way, free, thanks to them.

They were prostitutes. But I didn't want to judge them. Besides, why judge, by what right? The most despicable, most pathetic being was me. The most horribly alone was me. In Jeddah, it was worse: loneliness day and night. Around me, there were only men. Just men. I'm not homophobic. I have nothing against homosexuals. But I need women, myself, all women. In Saudi Arabia, they don't exist. Fortunately, in Cairo, there were the Moroccan women. With them my life had meaning. Money, I earned to give to them. It was only fair. I received much more in return. Much more.

I had a small apartment not far from the center of town. In the Dokki neighborhood. Next to a movie theater. I rented it all year round.

It was my nest for love, sex, and debauchery that I made no secret of. The concierge protected me. More precisely, he made sure my reputation as a womanizer didn't cause too much trouble in the neighborhood.

I paid him well too. He liked me a lot for that. And hated Moroccan women. "They're all whores with no religion," he repeated.

Who ever said they weren't?

Later, when Slima and her son moved into the apartment, the concierge declared war on me. It lasted two months. I hadn't checked with him, I hadn't asked his opinion.

Slima managed to bring him around.

Slima had a heart. Smashed to pieces, yes, but still capable of tenderness toward others, the world. She was no longer beautiful. She was ten years younger than me. Thirty-five.

She was going to get out of the business. She had been preparing to do so for several months, but didn't dare leave the world of magical Moroccan "girls," in exile and distress, free and perpetually adrift. Their stories never end well. She didn't know where to go next.

Morocco?

She had turned her back on it forever.

Her son?

She didn't recognize him. He was sixteen then.

She hadn't seen him for three years—the time she'd spent in a Moroccan prison.

Just before she was locked up in one of the worst prisons

in the world, she had time to go see one of her wealthy clients and begged him to help her son leave Morocco. Very old and very tender, the client took pity on her. It was he who advised Slima to send her son to Cairo, where he knew a lot of Moroccan prostitutes in exile. He would ask one of them, Lalla Fatma, to take care of Jallal. Of course, Slima would have to pay for this tremendous favour. Half of what she earned her first year in Cairo went to Lalla Fatma. After all, it was she who had watched over her son, his health, his morale. Who'd kept him alive.

Three years of separation. Three years of Slima without Jallal, and Jallal without Slima. A gulf had developed. Slima no longer knew how to touch her son. Jallal lived with his mother without knowing what to do or say.

Sixteen. He'd become a little man. He was taller than his mother. And the questions he asked himself were different from his mother's—about life, the future, the afterlife and loneliness. He was moving toward another world that I would only discover later. After Slima. Without Slima.

It was she who approached me at the Hotel Semiramis.

She left her Moroccan friends. Without so much as a glance at any other man in the casino, she came to me.

She didn't utter a single word, just looked at me straight in the eye, without playing coy.

No, she did not sell herself. She gave herself to me.

That was clear. She did not make herself out to be something she wasn't.

There was nothing vulgar about her. Nothing cheap. A woman prostitute, completely unashamed.

A woman who knew men, humanity, better than anyone. In sex. Beyond sex.

Her actions were unpredictable. Her gaze came from somewhere far, far away. Her tired body was still caught up in life's momentum, in spite of everything.

The night brought us together. Cairo was our little homeland.

I was happy, did not resist. I spoke first.

To amuse her, I introduced myself using my Arabic name, Mouad. The one my colleagues in Saudi Arabia gave me. I reinvented myself as Muslim. Without knowing it, I was converting to Islam, a little.

She believed me. I never dared to tell her the truth. For her I remained Muslim. That made things easier later. Getting married in Cairo. Obtaining a Belgian passport for her, another for Jallal. And then traveling. Going to Mecca.

She didn't tell me everything about her past. The story behind her terrible scars. Her Morocco. Her omissions.

Living with me as my wife, she remained true to her Moroccan sisters, the local prostitutes, women in need and on the run. She went to visit them once in a while. Even when she decided to wear the veil, the bond with them was never severed. Quite the contrary.

Everything happened very quickly. She came into my life. Two years later, she was gone.

And meanwhile, Jallal became my son.

Hard to believe, isn't it? The story's difficult to tell.

Where do I start, pick up where I left off?

I met a woman. I fell in love with her for reasons that elude me. Reasons I still don't know today.

She didn't make me a weakling, a housebroken man. Ring on his finger, a little anesthetized dog, as we say in Cairo when a man is under his wife's thumb. She didn't betwitch me. Didn't force me to marry her or prevent me from seeing other women.

It was like an interlude in a dream. A book of legends, a single legend.

Fate decreed I would play a role in the life of this woman on her way to another world.

A woman at the end of a cycle of her life on earth.

I chose nothing. I was driven. Guided.

I found another kind of love. Part of a new spirituality, Islam.

I even prayed. Five times a day. Like a good Muslim. A pious devotee.

It was good exercise.

I liked it. I enjoyed the daily cleanliness of the precepts of Islam. Slima taught me how to do my ablutions properly before each prayer. She helped me memorize the verses from the Koran to say during prayer. Showed me how to bend, stand up, kneel. What to begin with. What to end with.

She had all that in her. Muslim prayer. Very early in the morning. At noon, just before lunch. In the middle of the afternoon. At sunset. When the night was completely black.

I saw her do it. Out of love, I imitated her. Accompanied her. I went to the mosque with her once a week.

After just a month, the gymnastics of Muslim prayer held no more secrets for me and, miracle of miracles, did me as much good as they did her. A world of good. Like going to the pool every day when I was a teenager. It was the same kind of state. The same feeling. The same effect, physical and mental. A glow of happiness. Of euphoria. The mind calm and light. A white cloud in the blue sky after rain.

Soon, an addiction.

Especially for her. More and more, for her.

I ALWAYS DIVIDED my time between Jeddah and Cairo.

Every time, on my return, Slima took me deep into spirituality, into love through God.

Of course, none of this was totally free of contradiction or strange behavior on the part of Slima. Her gestures were sometimes bizarre. She often uttered high-pitched cries. But I couldn't help but see that she was genuinely inspired, inhabited by forces greater than her.

"We'll learn to love God, Mouad, to find Him again inside us. To do that, all I have are words in Arabic, the teachings of Islam. We'll use them. But we won't let ourselves become locked inside them. We'll find an answer in them. Or not. Of peace. Or not. But one thing is certain, we'll raise ourselves through our minds and bodies. Reach the sky. Swim in the sky. We're just like other Muslims but not quite like them. Only you and I know it. We will reinvent the religion, use it to question our relationship with the world and other people, with God, again and again. I don't want to force you. I don't want you to judge me. My life, this first life, is ending. The end is very near. I've found a path. I hear the voice. I'm answering the call. I can't do otherwise. I am a body. And not only a body. I've suffered too much. I'm not ashamed of my past. I don't deny my past. I stay on the same path, nothing more. Like my mother Saâdia, who adopted me in the mausoleum of the saint of Rhamna. In my own way but like her, too.

You said your name, Mouad, and I knew the time had come. That I had no time left.

Through you, Mouad, the Mystery is revealed to me.

I have only the words of Islam to help me reach the next stage, grasp its meaning, progress, listen. Love. Love.

I love you, Mouad. Do you believe me?

I love you, Mouad. You are my savior, my last road.

I love you and, through you, I love Him.

I believe. Finally, I believe.

I don't want to close my eyes anymore. I have the truth between my hands, in my heart. I can no longer turn my head away, pretend.

My body is His.

My soul is His.

He's there. Where you came from. Jeddah. Mecca. The desert.

I'm not Muslim.

I'm not only Muslim.

And I don't know what you are. Or why you're following me. Or rather, if. This must be love. Truly love.

Love.

Do you hear me, Mouad? Do you understand? I don't deny anything. I deny nothing. I'm going to Him. I'm close to Him. Darkness doesn't scare me anymore. Earth isn't my only home now, my only garden. Other places are being revealed. Other earths. Other nights.

The Door opens, a little at a time. A puff of air comes in. The hour of meeting is near.

I have to go into that desert. Walk in His footsteps. I know exactly where I'll find them.

I have a vision.

I see. I see.

I won't leave alone.

I'll leave a mark on this earth. A memory. Legacy. Son. Jallal.

Hold my hand, Mouad. I'm trembling.

He is real, he is real. Beyond the Red Sea I must go.

I see myself naked.

I'm not wearing anything.

The veils and masks I was forced to wear all my life are of no use anymore.

I'm not crazy. I know you know that. You come from far away, from another world, another culture, other customs. But you're like me, a human being. A human being.

You are my brother. I'm your sister. I live again. I am reborn. I'm leaving. I'm changing. For your eyes, your desire, your enthusiasm, your sex, your skin, your smell, your mystery. Your silence. God who is in you.

God who is in you."

I WAS ONLY A SERVANT in this story. The story of Slima. A passenger. A sidekick.

I learned, too. So much. About myself. Learned to find myself again. Hang in the air. Let go.

I helped her, Slima. Of course. I had to.

We went to Mecca, as she wished.

It was at the end of the two years we'd spent in Cairo.

We walked for two months in the desert of Mecca.

We started with the lesser pilgrimage, Al-Umrah.

We found an instructor there who showed us the way. How to circle the Kaibab. What to say. Where to rest, to sleep. Where to meet God and His prophet.

These very complicated rites of the first two days are impossible without a guide. On the third day, he said:

"You don't need me anymore. God will guide you. Go in purity. He is there. There. And there. Walk. Fly. Sleep. Breathe. Look. Lie down. Close your eyes. He is there. Everywhere. You'll see. You see Him already. You are right before His door."

In this man Slima had found a brother who spoke the same language.

I didn't understand everything. I was overwhelmed the entire time. Witnessing it all brought tears to my eyes. There before me, in Mecca, was all of humanity immersed in its most essential actions, searching for God, finding Him, speaking to Him, living and dying in Him day and night.

That astonishing spectacle, that immense fervor, connected me with a being deeply rooted inside me, whom I'd never even met.

I didn't understand what was happening to me.

I clung to Slima. She gave me her hand. She reminded me of what I had to say, the prayers and phrases to recite.

We entered into God together.

At that moment, yes, I was Muslim. Mouad. A Muslim surrounded by other Muslims. Muslim, and in another time.

Slima repeatedly fainted. To meet God in the blazing heat of Mecca, you have to be in good health, quickly acquire the knack of endurance. Know how to make your way through a very pious and sometimes very aggressive crowd. And most of all, avoid asceticism. That wasn't Slima's case. Long before Mecca, she'd decided to eat less. Food no longer interested her. Close to God, she consumed nothing but fruit juice. And constantly, the very cold water of the sacred well of Zamzam. It was cleansing her from the inside, she said, washing her heart, softening and soothing her. Changing her. Preparing her ever more.

Losing weight allows the soul to rise more quickly to God. It's a question of physics, of chemistry.

Slima was not wrong.

I followed her lead even in diet. I stopped eating. Like her, I shed weight day after day.

But I kept up my strength enough to take her in my arms when she fainted, eyes open.

In them I saw where she was going, rising. To the future. Hunger, God, and ecstasy.

My love for Slima greatly changed on that trip.

My love took on a new dimension.

I started to revere her. I understood why fate had put me on her path. My hand in hers. My heart open to spirituality, to something Arabic invented fourteen centuries ago so human beings could talk to the sky, and beyond the sky and horizon, behind the Darkness. Talk with the first light, its echo still visible. Look at the Kaaba, that huge dark room, and at once seize the opportunity to watch the universe swell and approach. To stop being afraid. To accept the desert. Kneel like Muslims and kiss the ground, respect it and never forget that this earth is inside us. It is us. We walk over ourselves. We eat ourselves. We enter ourselves. And sometimes, it's a miracle, we open ourselves to Mystery.

We see. We accept death. We go to it.

We learn History, starting from the first burst of light. It files with perfect clarity before us. Before Slima. Before me.

Slima barely spoke anymore.

She walked ahead but never let go of my hand. We slept together in a tiny room, she curled in the hollow of my body, I curled in the hollow of hers. Brother and sister. Muslims. More than that. Much more. And the opposite.

We dreamed in the same way. Beyond matter.

I spoke Arabic. I was no longer Belgian. I was no longer Western. Nor Arabic. Or a man of the twentieth century.

It was possible.

It's possible.

You can touch God. He might come to sleep between us.

He came to rest with us in the little room every night.

And I continued speaking Arabic. It became my first language.

Instead of Slima, I spoke with new words, buried in me from the start without my knowledge.

I was living another life. Slima made it possible.

That was her gift. Her promise. Her message.

After Mecca, we went to Medina. At the grave of the Prophet Mohammed, Slima wept for a day and a night, more overcome with emotion than I had ever seen her.

That is where I took leave of her. I could follow her to Mecca, intuitively, and take on her gestures and rise with her, but in Medina I could no longer be under the same sky.

I knew nothing of the prophet Mohamed, his life, his message. Slima had never really talked to me about the politician and warrior he had also been. We were immersed in the religion invented by this man without knowing who he really was. Of course there were his hadiths, but they were codified, rigid, too sacred.

In Medina, this abstract man became real—he had a grave.

Mohammed had truly existed. There, at Slima's side, I more or less had historical proof.

Slima, sincere believer and captive, tore herself weeping from her beloved messenger's grave and recited one of his hadiths. The last hadith. The one he spoke just before his death, the one his companions memorized.

The one about what the prophet Mohammed retained of his life, of life. Prayer. Fragrances. Women.

These elements were on the same level. One's meeting with God could go through these three stages that in essence were equal. I learned this hadith by heart too. For later, for the days of despair and sterile solitude.

In spite of myself, I remained separate, removed. And jealous. I couldn't go further. I could not love Mohammed as powerfully as Slima.

I dropped her hand.

Ecstatic, she remained at Mohammed's tomb.

That is where she fainted for the last time.

Dry-eyed, I buried her in the same city as her prophet.

That was her ultimate dream: to receive the grace of Mohamed. His earth. Touch the first holiness. Enter into it. Dissolve there. Explode there.

And alone I left for the desert, following the traces of my love for Slima. To finally realize what I had just experienced. Put words to this sublime love. Understand what had escaped me before. Walk a long time in the desert and its ruins. Meditate. Weep. At least try.

It took me several weeks to come back to earth.

In Cairo. Sleeping endlessly. Gradually relearning how to bear the emptiness of my life. Filling the days and nights in another way. Without her. Without her image, her eyes, her smell, her sex. Finally, I remembered that Slima had left me a legacy. A son. A promise. Jallal. A teenager. Lost and unknown, left on his own for too long in the terrible and intoxicating chaos of Cairo. He lived in the same apartment as me. But I didn't see him.

One morning, a year after Slima's death, I entered Jallal's room and I held out my hand. He replied with a little smile. Slima's at the casino in the Hotel Semiramis. Exactly the same.

III. Infidels

I

الله الرحمن الرحيم الملك القدوس السلام المؤمن المهيمن العزيز
الجبار المتكبر الخالق البارئ المصور الغفار القهار الوهاب الرزاق
الفتاح العليم القابض الباسط الخافض الرافع المعز المذل السميع
البصير الحكم العدل اللطيف الخبير الحليم العظيم الغفور الشكور
العلي الكبير الحفيظ المقيت الحسيب الجليل الكريم الرقيب المجيب
الواسع الحكيم الودود المجيد الباعث الشهيد الحق الوكيل القوي المتين
الولي الحميد المحصي المبدئ المعيد المحيي المميت الحي القيوم
الواجد الماجد الواحد الصمد القادر المقتدر المقدم المؤخر الاول الآخر
الظاهر الباطن الوالي المتعالي البر التواب المنتقم العفو الرؤوف
مالك الملك ذوالجلال والأكرام المقسط الجامع الغني المغني المانع
الضار النافع النور الهادي البديع الباقي الوارث الرشيد الصبور

2

Allah The All-Compassionate The All-Merciful The Absolute Ruler The Pure One The Source of Peace The Inspirer of Faith The Guardian The Victorious The Compeller The Greatest The Creator The Maker of Order The Shaper of Beauty The Forgiving The Subduer The Giver of All The Sustainer The Opener The Knower of All The Constrictor The Reliever The Abaser The Exalter The Bestower of Honors The Humiliator The Hearer of All The Seer of All The Judge The Just The Subtle One The All-Aware The Forbearing The Magnificent The Forgiver and Hider of Faults The Rewarder of Thankfulness The Highest The Greatest The Preserver The Nourisher The Accounter The Mighty The Generous The Watchful One The Responder to Prayer The All-Comprehending The Perfectly Wise The Loving One The Majestic One The Resurrector The Witness The Truth The Trustee The Possessor of All Strength The Forceful One The Governor The Praised One The Appraiser The Originator The Restorer The Giver of Life The Taker of Life The Ever Living One The Self-Existing One The Finder The Glorious The One, the All Inclusive, The Indivisible The Satisfier of All Needs The All Powerful The Creator of All Power The Expediter The Delayer The First The Last The Manifest One The Hidden One The Protecting Friend The Supreme One The Doer of Good The Guide to Repentance The Avenger The Forgiver The Clement The Owner of All The Lord of Majesty and Bounty The Equitable One The Gatherer The Rich One The Enricher The Preventer of Harm The Creator of The Harmful The Creator of Good The Light The Guide The Originator The Everlasting One The Inheritor of All The Righteous Teacher The Patient One

3

BY HEART. I made Mahmoud learn them by heart. All of them. The ninety-nine names of Allah. With the correct pronunciation. The correct rhythm. In classical Arabic.

He lay all day and night in his bed at Brugmann Hospital in Brussels. And he never took his eyes off me, clung to me like a baby who recognizes no one in the world but his mother.

"Jallal, my friend, my brother, say them again, the ninety-nine names. Again and again."

In truth, he knew them well, those sacred names. But in French.

Before, his name was Mathis.

Now he had an Arab name, Mahmoud, but didn't speak the language. That's what he told me.

We were patient.

I was very patient with him.

Our relationship lasted two months in all.

To experience everything with him, both Mathis and Mahmoud. As if it were the first day of my life. The last day of my life. To the point of total osmosis.

I taught him to write Arabic. I finally helped him enter that mysterious language—complicated, impossible, according to him. The language of his new religion.

For an entire night we studied the *alif*, the letter of all beginnings. *Alif* as an isolated letter at the beginning of a word, in the middle of a word, at the end of a word. How it's written, how it transforms. A letter, always the same and always different.

In the past, long before meeting me, *alif* had been a problem and had driven him to abandon the language in which one thing has multiple faces, multiple skins.

Why? Why the constant shifts? That perpetually elusive quality? Several languages within the same language?

I had no answers to these questions that I'd never asked myself. I didn't give much thought to Arabic. The language was in me long before there was a me.

I gave it to him as it was inside me.

I gave him what I knew and what I didn't.

He lay on his hospital bed. He always fixed me with a gaze both harsh and tender.

I didn't know how to respond to his gaze. But very quickly, I gave him my hand. Right from the third letter, *taa*.

I must be clear. I let him take my hand.

Taa caused him great fear. A panic attack. Suddenly he was no longer himself. The form of this letter, which he saw as a little basin with two hallucinating eyes, sent him back to a traumatic past I knew nothing about.

He took my left hand and squeezed it very hard.

I asked him if he wanted us to give up on *taa*. Closing his eyes, he said yes.

And we moved to the next letter.

Mahmoud was weak. So weak. He was leaving. Somewhere in his sick body, the pain was unbearable.

With my hand in his hand, he eventually passed out. Fell asleep. For a quarter of an hour.

My eyes did not leave his strange, white face. I put it all over inside me, inside my body and my soul.

Later *taa* became our letter. The letter symbolizing our connection, the dizzying things that were happening between us. The sacred things. We moved beyond the panic attack. We entered slowly into *taa* and left our mark there. Traces of ourselves.

He was the one who found the first word with *taa*. He was sleeping. He opened his eyes and he said the word. *Tawbah*.

How did he know that word? Where did it come to him from?

I didn't ask him these two questions. I didn't have time. He asked me:

"What does *tawbah* mean in Arabic?"

Strangely, I didn't know.

He repeated the question by adding a little detail at the end—my name.

"What does *tawbah* mean in Arabic, Jallal, my friend?"

To hear "Jallal" spoken in his soft voice helped me. He inspired me. I knew then what to say.

"To repent. To return to the true, the pure, the First."

"We'll both repent at the same time, won't we, Jallal? By the same near and far door that slowly opens before us."

His hand had not left mine.

Yes, we'll do things together, Mahmoud, I promise you. I swear.

I confirmed this pact without uttering a word. He hadn't said anything either. Everything happened in silence. Our eyes spoke for us.

I DIDN'T FORCE MYSELF to do anything with him. It was as if everything that happened between us was a matter of course.

Mahmoud was ill. I met him that way. And without a second thought, I caught his illness. I needed it. That illness and that love. Since I'd left Cairo with my mother's last husband, Mouad the Belgian, I'd searched Brussels for a savior. A soul to comfort me, understand me, guide me, make me lighter. A special being, a chosen being, a brother and a stranger. Mahmoud, ill, was this exceptional person. The visionary who forced me to drop everything and follow him in his view of the world, his way of loving, and his plan to leave his mark on earth.

I understood this from the start. As soon as I gazed into his eyes.

I didn't know Mahmoud. And nothing had prepared me to meet him.

For a year I'd been living alone in Mouad's apartment in Brussels. He had more or less abandoned me. He'd gone back to his job in Saudi Arabia. He felt that at my age, twenty-two, I was able to fend for myself in Brussels. In the West. He left me the apartment, too big for me, and sent me five hundred euros each month. On leaving, he told me: "It's time you became a man. Without me. You can't become a man sticking to me like glue. Do you understand?"

I understood nothing.

Meeting Mahmoud at Brugmann Hospital in Brussels helped me to understand. Not loneliness or abandonment, but the deep meaning of my life, my existence. With Mahmoud, sick and beautiful, frail and powerful, I'd found a mission. Love and a mission. To love and be angry. To finally get even with the world, which had never given me a thing and, what's more, had taken my mother, my Slima away from me. To give others a taste of the cruelty they'd instilled in me. The self-contempt they'd forced on me. To get my revenge. To avenge Slima.

Mahmoud was a stranger. I met him when I went to the hospital with Steve, Mouad the Belgian's nephew, who was an old friend of Mahmoud's.

Steve came to visit me at Mouad's apartment. He said: "Mouad called. He says hello. And he says you have to call him from time to time. He wants to know how you are. Are you doing alright?" I had nothing to say, either to Mouad or Steve, whom I barely knew.

Steve spoke again. "Mouad asked me to stop by once in a while. To get you out of the house. Do you want to do something? Catch a movie?"

We left the apartment together. Before the movie, we went to the Brugmann Hospital. Mahmoud was waiting for us. Waiting for me.

Steve had insisted, "It won't be long, Jallal. I have to visit him. He's not really a friend. We went to college together and apparently he's very ill. You don't mind coming?"

BETWEEN THE AGES of thirteen and sixteen, my mother Slima taken from me, I lived in Cairo in the care of Lalla Fatma.

She was abducted, tortured, imprisoned, damaged. She told me once, only once, about that disappearance, the unspeakable violence they'd inflicted upon her. She told me on the eve of her departure to Mecca with her husband Mouad.

Between the ages of sixteen and eighteen, years after Slima had left Morocco for Cairo, I was reunited with a mother who was no longer my mother, no longer capable of it. She didn't see me. She expected something else from life.

Slima had become a torn and shattered woman. Completely destroyed. Another person. But she was forced to keep working at her first profession, that of her mother and hundreds of thousands of other Moroccan women. Prostitution.

Quite in spite of myself, I became her friend. Her confidant. I pretended to be.

Before she joined me in Cairo, I had grown used to living without her. The endless din of the Egyptian capital was enough to fill me, to keep me away from my mother, away from the woman I still loved, but without understanding. In Cairo, by my side and at the same time absent, she talked politics quite often, too often. She was becoming part of another story, which didn't include me. She needed an ear. I played that role. She needed to retrieve her dignity in another way.

Her men, wealthy clients she met in posh Cairo hotels, paid for everything, including my schooling at the French Lycée.

I never really understood how, from her prison in southern Morocco, near Ouarzazate, she'd managed to have me sent to Cairo and into the care of Lalla Fatma, a Moroccan woman, a bit of a witch. How had she kept watching over me from that terrible, nameless prison far away?

I'll never know.

Even living under the same roof as my mother Slima again, I couldn't reconnect with her and our past in Morocco, in Salé. The hammam. The house in Hay Salam. The soldiers. The soldier. The movie, *River of No Return*.

Cairo possessed me. The crowds, twenty million, kept me company. Protected me. Separated me a little more each day from my mother Slima.

I learned solitude in Cairo.

Solitude in the midst of an angry but remote, unfeeling humanity.

I grew away from my mother.

I waited a year for her. For the first year, in Lalla Fatma's apartment, I still had hope and fervor, belief in her return. The second year, sad, heavy-hearted, I deliberately cut all ties between us. Every connection. Every last thread. I'd decided she was dead. She wouldn't be back. One day, someone would announce her death.

Just as well to kill my mother right away, let her go that very moment.

Adolescence is a time of power. Every day is a tragedy. Every day is war. We become ruthless. We forget quickly. Zap things quickly. Kill in cold blood. And keep on living. Without any guilt.

I became a monster.

Without my mother.

Even when she came back, her absence continued to haunt me. She really was another woman. In an opaque world.

We lived side by side. We drank the same water from the Nile. I saw nothing. I played the stupid boy. The blasé, vacant teen.

Desperate and fearful till the end, until death, living without her. Needy.

I'VE BEEN WITHOUT A MOTHER for ten years now.

I'm a little over twenty-three now.

I want to spit. Like when I was little, in Salé.

I walk the streets of Brussels. And I spit.

I look up at the black sky. And I spit.

I go to the door of Mouad's apartment. And I spit. I spit.

I remember what I told him, the man who accompanied my mother to her death in Medina, Saudi Arabia. "You're my father, Mouad, yes, yes," I told him several times to reassure him. He was falling asleep. "Yes, you can leave for Saudi Arabia with your mind at ease."

"I'm fine. I'm fine. I swear. You're right, I'm old enough to become a man. Twenty-two is the age of manhood. I'm a man, Mouad. I'm strong. I know my way very well around Brussels. I can manage alone. I'll go back to university. Yes, yes. This time you can believe me. You did what you could for me. You saved me. Thanks to you, I have a roof over my head. I won't starve to death. You're right, I'm grown up now. You can go."

Just before entering the apartment in Brussels, I hawk and spit.

I lied to Mouad. All I did was lie, wear a new mask every day. Brussels is killing me. Smothers me. Never talks to me.

Where am I? What am I doing here? How do you read the codes of this city? How do you approach people, read the signs? How do you live without color?

I spit. Again and again.

Spit renewed I renew my ties with childhood. With the ill-mannered boy I was in the city of Salé.

Brussels makes me want to close all the windows and all the doors. To become ill. End it once and for all. Escape, cross the river. Join my mother.

And that's what happened when Steve, who wanted to take me to the movies, took me first to Brugmann Hospital to visit a school friend of his. A Belgian, four or five years older than me, who was a patient there.

His name was Mathis. But like Mouad, he'd changed his name and religion.

A coincidence?

Later I understood that it was anything but a coincidence. Without having decided to do so, I'd followed my mother's road. Like her, I met a Belgian convert to Islam who would play the role in my life that Mouad had played in hers. With him, I entered the Revolution. With him, Mahmoud, I understood that a huge sacrifice had to be made in order for the world to change, for my heart to open and let in the light.

Mahmoud was in his hospital bed. In another bed, next to his, was an old man.

Mouad's nephew had brought flowers.

I'd brought a single candle, small and white. Bought long ago in Cairo. I had told myself that if this unknown sick person was nice, I'd give it to him. If not, too bad for him.

He was not only nice. He was radiant. Sick and radiant. Sick and so peaceful.

So gentle. So gentle.

He was the brother I was desperately searching for in Brussels. I knew it right away. So did he.

I kept the candle for another day. I didn't dare give it to him in front of Steve, the gift that was so important to me and came from a town where my life was so different.

I said nothing in front of him that day.

As we were leaving, Steve and I shook hands with him.

He said:

"You'll come back to see me, won't you?"

It was not an order or a prayer. It was understood. A voice from On High. Neither of us had any choice.

I had to go back. To continue what had begun. Become close very quickly, he and I. And in some way reproduce, replay the story my mother lived with Mouad the Belgian at the end of her life.

Yes, I had to go back. Every day. Without Steve, of course. Without revealing anything to him. Without revealing that I'd made my decision long before Mahmoud shook my hand.

It was written in stone. The Cairo candle was for him.

Later, for the two of us.

At first, I didn't dare reply to his invitation. But after a few seconds, trembling, I uttered a little "yes."

"I'd be very happy to come back and see you!"

He had the power to say things, decide things. Enter deep inside me. Read my heart. My soul. Give me food and water.

I returned two days later. The old man was asleep.

Mahmoud said:

"Do you see the sky? Are you looking at it the right way? And the Moon?"

I answered:

"Here in Brussels, everything seems black to me. I don't have anything. I wander aimlessly. I don't see anything. There is no sky."

"That's not true, Jallal. The Moon is there. Always. You have to go beyond the blackness. Beyond the veils. You're wrong, Brussels isn't black."

I didn't dare contradict him.

And he made the following proposal:

"Do you want to climb up on the Moon? Do you want to? We'll cut it in half. Half for you and half for me."

I realized this was an initiation into Mahmoud's inner language, his way of using words, connecting them to each other, reinventing, breathing new life into them.

I made an effort. I answered him in kind, trying to be inspired like him:

"One day, Mahmoud, we'll find a tree together and carve the first letters of our names in the bark."

"In what language, Jallal?"

"Do you know Arabic?"

He'd converted to Islam a few years ago but he didn't know Arabic.

"Will you teach me, Jallal?"

"Here, in the hospital?"

"Yes, here in this room. I have to stay almost two more months."

I immediately accepted.

I had not spoken Arabic since my arrival in Brussels with Mouad the Belgian, but the language was still alive and strong in me. I was going to know it more and more deeply in the two months I had left on this earth.

Mahmoud continued speaking like a poet.

"And so we'll go the Moon. We'll ride the mythical winged horse, Buraq, like the prophet Mohammed. He'll take us there. We'll look for a tree and carve the first letters of our names in Arabic. What do you say?"

How could anyone resist?

I didn't resist. He was ill. It was important to make him happy.

After a moment of silence, he said my name. Jallal.

Following a silence of exactly the same length as his, I said his name. Mahmoud.

The next day, I started to teach him Arabic. To write and speak it.

The old man watched us. Sometimes he participated in these very special courses. And in that way, he joined us on the journey to the Moon. To the light.

It was Mahmoud who told me one day about the ninety-nine names of Allah in Islam.

I was not really a good Muslim but I still knew them by

heart. Quietly reciting, chanting every single one of them each day, brought you closer to God, of course, and kept death away.

I told Mahmoud all that.

"Are you afraid of death, Jallal?"

Yes, I was still afraid of death.

Not he.

"So each time you come here to see me, we'll say the ninety-nine names of Allah. I don't want you to die, Jallal. Not right away. You'll start. You'll chant a name. Then another. In Arabic. I'll follow you. And one day, we'll say them at the same time, from the same heart. Without opening our mouths. Just by looking into each other's eyes. Does that suit you?"

It suited me perfectly.

He knew how to sweep me away. Guide me. Carry me along with him into a new cycle of life.

When I was with him I forgot all the rest, the better to find myself.

Finally I loved God. Allah.

Mahmoud said:

"Where is God in you?"

I didn't know.

He said:

"Do you know of the poet Jalal al-Din Rumi?"

I didn't.

Three days later, I knew everything about him.

Jalal al-Din Rumi was a Muslim poet, Sufi, who lived in the thirteenth century. He celebrated God and love for God in his poems, which Mahmoud considered sublime and others considered too free, blasphemous.

"Read the poet Jalal al-Din Rumi. You will know God. You will know love. And you will come to me with greater understanding. Jalal al-Din Rumi will be our witness. The witness of our meeting. Our reunion with God, His Hidden Mystery, His Eternal Word."

Miracles exist.

Faith can return.

As it was for my mother at the end of her life, Islam could be something besides prohibitions on thinking, existing, freeing yourself.

Mahmoud and I gradually reinvented Islam. We found love there. Love. In our own small way, we made it progress.

I NEVER DARED TO ASK, "How did you come to Islam?"

One morning, after taking his many medications, he began to speak.

"I went to Afghanistan. I learned everything. Learned it again. I was a rookie journalist. It was an excuse to go there. I lived there for two years. I returned transformed. A different person. On my Belgian identity card I'm still Mathis. But since my Afghan emir chose Mahmoud as my name, I've given up my past life. I'm someone else now. Do you understand? Do you understand?"

Did I understand? What had he really been doing in Afghanistan? And who was this emir who'd revealed him to himself? A Taliban? An Islamist from another group? A terrorist? Was Mahmoud like that emir?

I kept my doubts to myself. It wasn't the time to share them, to talk about them.

It was my turn to speak.

"My mother died in Medina. Her last husband, Mouad, brought me back to Brussels. And he left. I can't do anything here. I'm horribly lonely here. None of it was my choice. Here everything looks black. This land is blackness. I want to go to the Moon with you. Ride the winged horse Buraq with you. Pass through the seventy thousand veils with you, the veils of light and darkness that separate us from the Creator. And take along the white candle I bought in Cairo."

He took the candle.

And he smiled. He looked like an angel. He was an angel.

"We'll go to the Moon. We won't be afraid of the dark ... Tonight you'll stay here, you'll sleep in my bed. I'll hide you. We'll light the candle in a secret corner. We'll wait. Finally the sky will open."

I hid in his arms. I slept, traveled, supported by his arms.

We never spoke of the past again. All that interested us were God, His Love, and the Moon.

I ENDED UP BUYING an orderly's apron. That way I could enter the hospital whenever I wanted.

The old man slept almost all the time. Dying a little more each day. He seemed to be at peace. He'd accepted the idea of the end. Of leaving. Across the sky. Mahmoud and I liked to watch him sleep; he was in some other place right beside us. Sometimes we witnessed the reawakening of his childhood fears. He was seized by panic though he was sound asleep.

He woke with a start. He quickly got out of bed. His arms flailed every which way, seeking a direction and finding it; a dark corner behind an empty little white cabinet, where he curled up in a ball. Clutched his head in his hands. And began to talk, whisper. Maybe pray.

The old man never wept. At that moment he was in a state of terror. Horror. Paralysis.

"Peace does not exist. Will never exist in us. We were wrong. We'll always, always be afraid."

The old man told us this as if pronouncing an oracle.

If his attacks came on when I was in the room, Mahmoud and I went to him without conferring. We each took one of his hands and talked to him. Every time, when he was back in bed, he asked for a lullaby. Mahmoud didn't know any. I still had the song in me somewhere faraway. *River of No Return.*

It was only when I found myself standing in front of his bed—empty, this time for good—that a slightly crude question crossed my mind.

What did he die from? What was his illness?

"He'd had cancer for several years. Widespread cancer."

I didn't dare pursue my curiosity to its logical conclusion.

What was that old man doing in the same room as Mahmoud?

Mahmoud had told me he was in hospital because of a car accident. He'd received a blow to the head. The doctors kept him under observation, just in case.

I'd believed him. I'd always believed him.

The death of the old gentleman helped me to finally understand. Mahmoud suffered from the same problem. Widespread cancer.

Allah is visible and hidden. Mahmoud too. He showed his inner truth and threw a veil over his profound suffering, his illness.

The old man's bed remained empty until the very end.

I slept as much as possible in the arms of my sweet and desperate patient.

I wasn't afraid.

I continued to sing. The ninety-nine names of Allah. *River of No Return* by Marilyn Monroe.

I discovered a passion in myself. Two passions. Love, reinvented. The ability to take care of another person. Assist him. Be him.

Without ever having learned how, I became a nurse. I knew what to do, naturally. Knew the right tone. The selflessness. The necessary attentiveness. Discreetly I watched the other nurses at the hospital. I envied them. I stole the things I didn't know from them to give to Mahmoud. To bring relief. A little relief. Love. More and more. And I accepted that I'd never really know everything about Mahmoud. Here. On this earth. In this life.

I'd found my place in Brussels. A small place. At last. A vocation. To touch. To heal. Take someone's hand. Feel their pulse, listen to their breathing. Draw closer to a heart. Listen to it. Follow its rhythm. Enter its mystery. Mahmoud's overwhelmed me. I was ready to follow him everywhere. To the end. Beyond the seventy thousand veils. Explode. Explode with love.

The two of us. Spreading the light. Entering into the light. Into the white. Into the farthest depths of darkness.

I've made my decision. I won't leave him. I've been growing attached to him. Since the beginning. Every day and every night a little more. I'll scream. I'll love. I'll become ill. Am already ill. Ill, and I'm leaving too. Mahmoud isn't forcing me. I'm leaving of my free will. With Mahmoud, I speak Arabic. I'm reunited with an origin. God. I give him the language. He takes it. He changes it. He returns it to me.

I was lost.

I found the way. Faith. Love. Death. Vengeance. The ultimate union. The sublime explosion.

In the terrible blackness of Brussels, I found Mahmoud. He is in me. He knows where to go. Where to sleep. Where to die. As brothers.

I followed him. I follow him. I have a brother. We are Muslims. Very soon we'll mount the winged horse Buraq. Flee Brussels. Go to the end of love. Stop doubting. My hand in Mahmoud's, to join my mother.

LONG BEFORE GOING into hospital, Mahmoud had carefully planned everything. His illness would not prevent him from going to the end of his mission. To plant a bomb where he was told to do so. Therefore, go to North Africa. Casablanca. Blow up. Destroy. Shock. And through this extreme act, speak. Make others speak. Leave a legacy. A message. Which?

I don't know if he was right to want to carry out an attack. I knew, however, that at some point we are forced to challenge, spit hard, stop being polite, stop being small. Do service. Sacrifice. Die violently for others. For Islam and its glory?

Mahmoud said:

"Not only for Islam."

For us, then? And who else?

I meditated on these questions for an entire sleepless night. Had I understood everything about Mahmoud and his mission? Did we have the same concept of Islam? Was I ready, confident and sincere, to go with Mahmoud to the end of his road of no return?

I couldn't answer that. And Mahmoud wasn't going to help me. But the blackness of Brussels was more than I could bear. The lack of my mother, great, immense. I had to find her by going down the same road as she had. Avenge her through an act of love. Avenge her on this earth that had hurt her so much. Morocco.

Inside me, everything was confused.

At Mahmoud's side, I saw clearly. I was going.

We felt no contradiction, then. Inside us, it all seemed true. Obvious. What other Muslims said, what they were going to say and do, judge us, cast aspersions on us, predict damnation for our souls, did not interest us. Did not concern us.

We were free now.

Free Muslims.

In the Brugmann Hospital room that protected us from the outside world, we prayed in earnest. Side-by-side. Facing Mecca. Facing my mother. Facing God. Accompanied by His ninety-nine names.

We recited the same suras of the Qur'an. The same phrases. The same magic words. Our movements synchronized. Standing. Doubled over. Standing again. Kneeling. Prostrated. Arms joined over the heart. Eyes open. Closed. Five times a day. Sometimes more.

MAHMOUD SAID THE DOCTOR had told him there was nothing more they could do. He was cured.

Really?

One day, we left.

The mission awaited us. I knew exactly what we would do. Carry out a suicide bombing somewhere in Casablanca. Kill ourselves. Certainly kill other people with us. Innocent people? But only Mahmoud knew the details, the steps to follow, the where and how.

Casablanca isn't far from Brussels. Just three hours by plane.

Mahmoud took care of everything. To reassure me, he told me it wasn't the first mission he'd been assigned in a city he didn't know at all. He knew where to go. How to get by. Get across Casablanca unnoticed. He had two addresses. One for the hotel where we'd stay a night. The other for a cyber café.

I trusted him, of course. Always. I continued to take his hand. Even in Morocco. He guided me in my own country. I didn't know anyone there anymore.

Casablanca had eight million Moroccans inside her, in her belly. They came from everywhere. Rif. Atlas. Fez. Taouirt. From Errachidia. Chaouia. Doukkala. Arabs. Berbers. Drunks. Power-mongers. Prostitutes. Lots of prostitutes. Lost souls. The jungle. Madness. Injustice everywhere, day and night. Arrogance. Perversion. The Money King. Crime as Law. Nothing romantic. Everything dirty. Everything rotten. Everything disappearing, collapsing. Everything failure. Everything closed. Including God's doors. Everything was murder. Murders. Casablanca was a vale of grief. More than any other place in Morocco, the city was permeated by deep and incurable sorrow. Hope no longer existed. Free, open Islam no longer existed. Love was unknown, alien and desperate.

That was our mission, to make people see love. Through death. Through an extreme act. Perform an action to make people think. To stand firm against the plague spreading through Morocco. Banality. Narrowmindeness. Confinement. Submission. Mired in falsity and ignorance. The programmed destruction of individuals, of people like my mother Slima who dare one day to try for freedom, resistance, a different road.

To rise up against an entire country.

An entire people.

Finally, to try to ask the real questions. Who brought us to this point, this state of collapse, this misfortune, this self-negation, this infectious blindness? Who is preventing our souls from taking flight and writing another History with a new messenger? Who is blocking us, turning us to stone and denying us the right to be what we are: men, standing?

The hotel where we were supposed to sleep the first night no longer existed. In its place was a gaping hole.

We went to the Hassan II Mosque. A grandiose monument, empty, adrift by the sea.

We hid inside.

It was there, in the darkness, in the night by the raging sea, that Mahmoud told me everything.

And, in detail, the plan for carrying out our mission.

How to prepare ourselves for death.

Perform our ablutions. The last ones. The ones for death.

The Hassan II Mosque was haunted. Its jinns were not Muslim. Its smell was strange, icy, cold, terrifying.

We were cold.

Mahmoud shivered all night. My arms and legs were not enough, I could not pass on what little heat that remained in my body. He was afraid. His teeth were chattering. He hadn't really recovered from his illness as he'd claimed.

I asked him to recall the ninety-nine names of Allah. To bring them to the front of his mind. Before his eyes.

He did.

I did the same.

In the black vastness of the mosque, I began. Quietly at first. Then more loudly. I said a name. He said the next one. Until the end.

And then we started again.

For an hour, maybe a little more, these sacred names reassured us, helped us to stop feeling the icy cold of the mosque, the emptiness of this mosque so loved and hated by Moroccans.

It was going to be a very long night. And apart from reciting the magical names, I didn't know what to fill it with, how to make it less harsh.

What could I do to help Mahmoud?

We sat on the ground facing each other. I could barely see him. But I sensed his warmth, his smell, his shadow.

I searched for his left hand. I found it. I took it, squeezed it in mine.

He searched for my left hand. I helped him find it, take it in his, talk to it.

The two of us formed a circle now.

I brought my head close to his. He did as I did.

He touched my forehead. I touched his.

Our heads were joined.

He entered me.

I entered him.

We stayed this way for some time, united, communing, waiting for what would happen next, what the night would bring. In the same direction. A single body.

Suddenly he raised his head and without releasing my hand, he stood.

He'd received a signal. An inspiration. Someone was speaking to him.

Without thinking, I followed his movement toward the sky.

I got to my feet at almost the same moment. I drew closer to him. He was cold again. His teeth chattered. I took him in my arms. He let me.

He whispered in my ear:

"Say your mother's name!"

Slima.

"Five times!"

Slima. Slima. Slima. Slima. Slima.

He was inventing a ritual.

Now I searched for his ear.

"Say the name of your mother five times!"

Denise. Denise. Denise. Denise. Denise.

"Say my name now, my new name! Five times!"

Mahmoud. Mahmoud. Mahmoud. Mahmoud. Mahmoud.

"Now you say my name! The name I've always had! Five times!"

Jallal. Jallal. Jallal. Jallal. Jallal.

He bent down and kissed my feet. He gave each foot five kisses.

He rose again.

Now I bent down too. I found his bare feet. And I kissed them five times.

When I stood up, he wasn't there anymore. He'd disappeared into the darkness.

A great fear invaded my entire being. An extreme solitude. An urgent longing to cry my heart out.

I'm going to die alone. I'm going to die alone.

A voice called out. It came from everywhere.

"Turn around!"

It was his voice, a little elated.

"Raise your arms in prayer, and spin. Around and around in circles. Now spin around me."

Darkness and cold still reigned in the Mosque of Hassan II. I still didn't see Mahmoud.

"Where are you? Mahmoud, where are you?"

After a moment of silence that seemed an eternity, the answer came from afar.

"Spin, Jallal. Around and around. Spin like me. Around and around in circles, and come to me."

I raised my arms to heaven, to God. I still saw nothing. Mahmoud's voice was my only guide.

"Come . . . come . . . Around and around in circles . . ."

I followed.

I turned slowly, without moving from the place where I was standing.

I felt nauseous almost right away. I nearly stopped and vomited.

Mahmoud's voice came again. In a trance. Soft. Violent. Female. Male.

"Spin . . . Spin . . . Don't stop . . . Around and around . . . And come to me . . . I'm coming to you . . . Spin . . . Open yourself . . . Open up . . ."

I forgot my pain. I continued spinning. And moving across the floor.

Suddenly the darkness no longer existed. Like Mahmoud, undoubtedly, I'd decided to close my eyes.

We danced all night. We chanted the ninety-nine names of Allah without stopping. I searched for him. He searched for me. We brushed against each other. We met. We separated.

Our voices guided us throughout the endless night. Our bodies no longer existed. Union was possible, Mahmoud was right.

There were three of us. We were at the very beginning. Light would burst forth. A great explosion. A great echo. Two bodies. A single force.

We climbed very high, beyond seventh heaven, and pushed past all the boundaries, all religions, all sexes. We became stones, clouds, stars, galaxies. We saw everything. Listened to everything. History was revealed to us. The Hand of God appeared. His face came closer to us. A breath of fresh air carried us along. Spinning had become our way of being, of communicating, penetrating each other. Spinning without stopping. Until the ultimate intoxication. The ultimate union. Death.

Faith is beautiful. God calls out to us. We were sleeping.

THE NEXT MORNING when I woke up, Mahmoud was staring at the explosive belts on the ground.

"Don't be afraid, Jallal. Come. Look. The belts will help us carry out our plan, our journey."

Where had he found them?

While you were sleeping, I went to get them from one of our faithful. A sleeper agent. He lives in a miserable douar. The Chechnya shanty town. Do you know that douar? Have you ever heard of it?"

I hadn't.

I went to the explosive belts and with no hesitation touched them.

Then we went to the hammam. It was empty.

I let Mahmoud wash me. I lay on the hot ground and gave my body to his hands. They knew what to do. Redrawing my body. My being.

Then I did the same for him. I reproduced his actions detail for detail. His itinerary.

We weren't washing because we were dirty. We were preparing for the final journey.

Before leaving the hammam, in a dark corner of the rest room, we got dressed and we put the explosive belts around our waists.

It was Friday. We wouldn't go pray. There was no point.

Later, the prophets would pray for us. Somewhere in Casablanca, we had to go blow ourselves up. Burn. Pass on the message we'd received.

Everything must be destroyed.

We didn't yet know exactly where and when to perform the sacrifice. Act of vengeance. Sound the alarm. Die of love.

Mahmoud took me to a cyber cafe downtown, not far from the Café de France.

It was 11:30.

He logged on to a strange site. The words were written in Arabic letters but I didn't understand them. Persian? Hindi?

I was sitting next to him. I saw everything. And I understood. It was an Islamist website. I looked away for a moment. Now I had confirmation that Mahmoud had another mission. Apart from ours.

He was sick. Dying. That's why they'd chosen him.

He knew Arabic. To keep me, he'd pretended not to. I was teaching him what he already knew, what he already mastered perfectly.

Was he a traitor?

Why had he lied to me? Why hadn't he told me he was an Islamist, as I'd suspected for one fleeting moment? Why hadn't he told me clearly and frankly that he'd been assigned a mission that had nothing to do with the plan we shared, our sublime explosion?

Why was he using me this way?

By following Mahmoud, had I unknowingly become an Islamist terrorist too?

How could I keep following this path? With him? Without him? And what could I do with my disappointed, bruised heart?

A thousand contradictory questions invaded my mind at that moment. I kept them to myself.

Suddenly I was afraid of Mahmoud and all he'd never told me about his past.

Who was he really? What had he really understood and retained about Islam? Was that what Islam was, this plan for terrorism, not for love?

I lowered my head. An unknown sadness took hold of me. A dizzying uncertainty. An unfamiliar abyss. And also an urgent desire. To spit. Spit hard. From anger. Disillusionment. Distress.

What was I to Mahmoud? Did he really love me? Was he the saint that I'd seen in him, imagined him as?

He very quickly realized what was going through my head. The questions. The bitterness. The desire to flee. Give up. Close the door.

While searching the Islamist website for the secret message, he took my left hand. Gentle. Love.

I looked up at him. He looked at me, waiting for me, his tear-filled eyes watching over me.

Bewitched by his aura, almost divine, and everything powerful and magnificent emanating from him, I closed my eyes to what I'd discovered about the ideology that stood between us. I forced myself to find my truth again, our truth. Our trust. The fond memory of the bed at Brugmann Hospital in Brussels, where we met and learned to reveal ourselves to each other, naked and sincere.

How could I have doubted him, doubted his love for me? I was the traitor, not he. Not him. I was ashamed.

Now it was clear. He was an Islamist terrorist. The real thing. Programmed that way for a very long time. But meeting me, without dropping the initial plan made with people I knew nothing about, his thinking changed. Exploding at my side took on another meaning. A friend and brother, he would accompany me right to the bitter end of my desire for vengeance on the people who had destroyed my mother Slima. He would return to the light with me. My mother's light.

Despite the waves of doubt bearing down one after another on me, on my heart, I kept walking down the path invented by Mahmoud and me. On a bed. A drifting raft.

That's what Mahmoud's eyes were saying to me.

Moved, I gazed into their depths. Tasted their tears. Loved their light.

Everything had been decided. Why speak of it again, stop or hesitate?

Mahmoud moved a little closer. He reassured me.

"Death is not death. Do you know that?"

I didn't know. I believed it—believed him—now.

"You won't be alone, Jallal. We won't be separated. It's in the contract. I insisted on it. I'm with you. I'm yours."

These last words seemed cold.

He added:

"You know better than me, Jallal. It's you who will open the door of the sky for us. You. Not me."

I couldn't think anymore. I didn't know how to think. Or go back in time. I was overwhelmed. But Mahmoud's words helped me regain my self-control and stop hesitating. Stop baulking at the borders of the known, the visible. Give myself to Mahmoud and the mad, suicidal power that had taken hold of us.

Trembling from head to foot, I said:

"I believe. I believe in us. I believe in you. You are my God. My religion. You're mine. I'm yours. Let's go . . ."

Just as we were leaving the café, the owner blocked our way.

"I know everything. I received an alert. You were logged onto a very dangerous site. I know where you're going. I called the police. They'll be here any moment. Stay calm and no one will get hurt. Go to the back of the shop . . . Go . . ."

Without a word we went to the back of the cyber café. Three boys were still there, glued to their screens. The owner ordered them to get out, fast! He tried to shut us in by lowering the metal blind.

I didn't have time to think. Or be afraid. It all happened very quickly.

Mahmoud took my hand, we looked at each other and made a run for it.

We jumped on the owner. The blind was half down, the owner on the floor. Mahmoud gave him a blow to the head and I gave him one in the gut.

He passed out.

We went out the door. To our great surprise, a large crowd was waiting.

One of the three boys who'd been in the café shouted:

"It's them, the terrorists! Terrorists and fags ... See? Look under their clothes ... They've got explosive belts ... Look! ..."

The crowd looked at us.

We looked at the crowd.

For an eternity.

Just like in the movies.

What were we going to do?

Mahmoud found a solution. He shouted:

"Stand back! Stand back! ... We're not fags ... We're brothers ... Stand back, or we blow up our belts! ... You'll all die with us ... Stand back! ... Stand back ... We're not fags ... We're brothers ... Two brothers joined by Love ... God is with us ..."

He was strong, firm, fair. A leader.

The crowd, who understood he wasn't joking, took off in a flash.

Sudden emptiness. The sea. The ocean. A door in the distance slowly opening.

We ran. All across Casablanca. Ran. Ran. To hide?

The police were closing in on us. By now, through rumors and the media, probably all of Morocco knew of and was following our flight, the whole country wondering the same thing we were.

Where were we going to blow ourselves up?

Certainly not at the place indicated on the Islamist website that Mahmoud had consulted. Now everyone knew where it was.

Then where?

We didn't talk.

There was nothing more to say.

That great big city of eight million people was empty. Completely. Totally. It was afraid. Of us.

We kept running.

Police sirens were everywhere, followed us everywhere.

And then, without a word, we headed to the mosque of Hassan II.

It was a bad idea, of course. During the day, it was heavily guarded.

We stopped.

We were cornered. The sirens were getting closer. The world was closing in on us. Failure closing in.

What could we do?

A miracle, my God! A miracle! Now! Now!

An abandoned movie theater saved us. It was me who spotted it. It looked exactly like the one from my childhood, in Salé. The An-Nasr cinema. The Victory Theatre.

Nobody saw us go in the back door.

It was dirty inside. Dirty, dark, peaceful. Inhabited. Haunted.

We dropped slowly and gently to the floor. Exhausted. Completely spent. Terror in our hearts. Still together.

And oddly, we fell asleep. Out like a light. Both of us.

It was the end. The real end. Behind the curtain. The white screen took in neither shadows nor images now. We could leave. Now. Just the two of us. Mahmoud. Jallal. Mahmoud and Jallal. Without taking anyone with us. Taking nothing but the memories we shared. Failing in Mahmoud's terrorist mission. Mad with Love, succeeding in ours.

The winged horse descended from heaven. Silent and unreal, mythical Buraq, waiting in the darkness of the theater.

I had a dream. I saw a movie. The same one as always. *River of No Return*. For the first time in a movie theater.

Mahmoud joined me in the dream. We sang the song from the movie twice, and went to look for my mother, the soldier, and ourselves in another life.

But also in the dream, just before leaving on this new journey, we accomplished our mission. We delivered the message. Morocco knew now. People knew us. Through our courage, our faith, our love and despair.

We speak another language, but we are not madmen.

We are two brothers.

Two names in Arabic.

Mahmoud and Jallal.

Osmosis. Poem. Breath. Heart. Fire.

The sublime explosion will occur.

We won't kill anyone.

Nobody will get hurt.

The theater was very dark.

In a single movement, twins in a single body, two strangers in one faith, one God, we created the light.

Boooom!

Booooom!

BOOOOOOOOOOOOMMMMMM!

IV. God

MY DEAR CHILDREN, COME IN. I was expecting you. Come, both of you. Don't be shy. No need to pretend or be afraid here. You've arrived. You've crossed the river. I followed you. I've been with you from the start. Approach. Approach. Closer, closer. Boundaries no longer exist. Behind me, the other world begins. In front of me, you must not lower your eyes. Look up. Look up. Higher. Higher still. That's it, look at me as I look at you. Love me as I love you.

Take off your clothes. They're of no more use here.

Take them off. All of them.

Shame does not exist. No longer exists.

Jallal, join hands with Mahmoud.

Mahmoud, that's what I'll call you from now on. That's what you wanted. We'll forget about Mathis, is that it? Yes? No? You're not sure?

All right, then, in this world you'll be both. Mahmoud and Mathis. Mathis-Mahmoud. Mahmoud-Mathis. Does that suit you? You won't have to choose, give anything up, split yourself in two.

I knew your two lives. I will judge you on both. You became Muslim, but that's not what saved you. I will look into your heart and make a decision. I know your soul. I took it from you and I'm giving it back. Come closer! You too, Jallal!

Voilà. You've decided to be brothers. You left the other world as brothers. Mathis was the strongest. The most determined. But you expected nothing less from him, isn't that true Jallal? Isn't it? His strength guided you, gave meaning to the chaos of your life, the darkness of your solitude, the misfortunes always close behind you.

You found a heart, Jallal.

You are that heart, Mathis.

You didn't wait for me. You came together without me, without my blessing. And you were right. I gave you each a heart. It beats inside you without my intervention. It is your heart that decides, that speaks on your behalf. On my behalf. Yes, you did the right thing. I created fate. Yours snuck by me. I must have been sleeping. You took that power. You decided to join your two hearts forever. Sacred Union. Single heart.

Even hidden, I see it before me. It continues to beat for you both. Here that heart will never stop.

Don't cry, Jallal. There's no reason to cry anymore. Or, if you want to cry, but only for joy. The clouds are below. Can't you see them?

Dry your tears. Do it. So I can continue. Other hearts await me. And they're far from being as serene as yours.

Mathis, help him dry those tears.

Here you can finally know each other. Know each other naked. Know each other without judgments or insults. No houris or virgins for you. I'll make sure you're left alone. For as long as you wish.

Another day you'll see familiar faces, people close to you. They're already here. They're resting too. Taking time for themselves. The sky is mesmerizing, disorienting. Go off on your own together as much as you want.

Eternity begins here. Now.

Don't worry, Jallal, the earth below continues to turn. The Apocalypse is not on our doorstep. Your childhood hero Robocop is aware of your arrival. But not the actor who played him, Peter Weller, no. He's living down below, for now.

The soldier's here too. Has been for a very long time. Alone. Always alone. He's still not over the trauma of war.

Slima your mother met him once. She prefers not to see him again. She spends her time praying, writing poems, talking with her own mother, the woman who adopted her, Saâdia.

She's waiting for Mouad her husband to arrive.

I know Jallal. I know you don't like Mouad. You'll have time to get rid of that resentment. He's not a bad man. Soon you'll see.

Are you still crying? Come, now! Why? Do *you* know, Mathis? You're afraid, Jallal? You mustn't be.

Give me your hands. Yes, like that, both of you. Close your eyes.

I give you my blessing. I send a breeze of purity over and into your hearts. Let it win you over, transform you, transport you. You'll never be separated here. Never judged. Your bond is eternal.

Mahmoud take Jallal in your arms!

Jallal take Mahmoud in your arms!

Now, each blow gently on the other's neck and nape!

Go ahead. Don't be shy. Blow hard and gently.

That's right.

Go, now, go and explore your new life. Sleep if you want. Whenever you want. Day and night are the same thing here.

No, you don't want to leave? To sleep? You prefer to stay with me? But I've got work to do. Other souls are coming up. They're arriving. Look behind you! They're growing impatient. I must be there for them. On time. Do you understand? Yes? No?

What exactly do you want?

Another prayer? Another blessing? Stories? A story? Just one story? You want to know me better?

I'm here in front of you. You can look at me. I exist. As you can see. That's not enough for you? What do you want? A poem? A dance of celebration? A *youyou*?

A story? Is that what you want? You really insist?

Then listen. I'll tell you about *my* first life.

I was born in America. I never knew my father. So who gave me life? I'll never know. I lived without him, without trying to find out who he was. To find him.

My mother? She was taken from me very early. When I was around the age of three. I don't remember what she looked like anymore. Only her smell. She almost never washed. She was sick. She had serious fits. She had a mental illness. She was there and then she wasn't. Didn't see me anymore. Couldn't look after me anymore. I never complained. I loved my mother, even when she was sick. I adored her even negligent. She gave me what she could. I didn't cry. I watched her all the time. I clung to her, never left her side. The world wasn't kind to her.

Women always need to do more, prove themselves more. Give more. More and more. And never any gratitude. Selfless acts. A sincerely understanding heart. My mother was required to be a woman, mother, lover, worker, servile and submissive . . . She couldn't do it. The world was no place for her. She didn't have the strength to keep acting in an absurd comedy. Wearing one mask after another. So she fell asleep. She never left the bed. I slipped in beside her. Inside her. There was no more food. We gave ourselves to each other, fed off each other. I had her empty breast in my mouth all the time. I didn't need milk. I understood. I accepted her decision. What was the point of living? She was doomed from the start. Why resist? To prolong life, my life, her daughter's life? At three years old, I'd already had enough, there was nothing I hadn't felt. I clung to her in the dirty little bed, in her weak arms. I listened to her heart. Its beating reassured me. It told me not to be afraid of death. Something comes after, something is there. Boom. Boom. Boom. I can still hear it. The world through the boom-boom of my mother's heart. It will never stop. I hear it. Do you hear it too?

One day they came to take her away. People told me later: "Your mother's crazy, forget about her!"

Forget? What were they talking about? And who were these heartless people giving me the order?

I never understood what other world they'd sent her to. Of course I've looked for her here in heaven. She's not here. Where is she? Still alive down on earth? It's possible.

I grew up in need. Without knowing how to protect myself. Without knowing how to be a woman.

I remained stuck in that time. A child.

Look at me. Don't you agree? What do you see? A child. No?

You don't have to answer.

And then?

After that, only images. And images. Adulation. The void. I walked. I jumped. I wandered. I naively tried to understand. I tried to educate myself, but that didn't help. Right from the start, the world denied me any chance to make it through, to get a taste of peace or enduring love.

So, there it is. Is that enough?

What do you want now? What happens next?

You already know. That, you can guess. I was sent to live with people. Families. Strangers. Faces with no light in them. All indifferent. They quickly tired of me. Every summer, a new family. A new place. New Orleans. Savannah. San Diego. San Francisco. Los Angeles. I never really knew where I was, what house, what neighborhood I was in, how I was supposed to go in and out. In every place, I was shut in. I didn't recognize anything. Nothing. Only the darkness of night, where I could find my mother again, calmed me a little.

During the school year, I was sent to orphanages.

The "homes." I was a girl from "homes." "She comes from 'homes,' the tall little girl over there. She has no parents. She's a shameless hussy." That's what the other students said about me. Horrible! They were all very mean. Absolutely all of them. At the time, the Authorities mixed orphanage children with ordinary children without asking too many questions. What a mistake! What suffering! What shame!

I don't know how I got through it, how I didn't go crazy, join my mother.

I don't know how people resist the haunting temptation of killing themselves. What held me back? I was barely ten years old and I already thought about that.. About killing myself. Leaving the world. Going back to my mother's dry and empty breast.

Some people said she was dead. I never believed them. For me she was in heaven, up in the sky. For me, heaven up in the sky was no metaphor. It was real. "My mother lives in the sky." When I revealed this secret, people laughed at me. "That clumsy clot from 'the homes' says her mother is in the sky! She's naive and simple-minded, that girl, nothing will ever come of her."

I am nothing. They were right. I let everything go. People could do what they wanted with me and my body.

They didn't hold back. The whole world raped me. No one has ever understood anything. No one. No one protested, defended me, gave me back my humanity.

I was a body I didn't live in. Not anymore.

The idea and possibility of salvation never crossed my mind.

With time, I became an erotic image for them. A cut-rate fantasy, open to all. A sex. A whore for the entire world. I made movies. I changed my name. I danced. I sang. *I'm Through with Love. I Wanna Be Loved by You. River of No Return.* They understood nothing. I understood nothing. I tried so many times to understand the things that human beings considered important. Culture. Books. Michelangelo. Leopardi. James Joyce. William Faulkner. Omar Khayyam. Gibran Khalil Gibran. Tintoretto. Stanislavski. I don't know if any of it helped me to find myself or just made me more lost, drifting farther away from everything, everything.

I wrote. Bits and pieces. The poems of an unhappy little girl. A little girl for eternity. I sent them to an actor who was like a father to me in my teenage dreams. Clark Gable. I don't know if he ever got them. When we shot *The Misfits* together, directed by John Huston, he never mentioned them. Was he wrong about me too?

I screamed a lot in that last movie. I was at the end of my tether. My suffering was at its peak. It was there, in that huge, clean desert where we were shooting, that I heard a voice. The Voice. It gave me a message.

I had been chosen.

I'd been chosen? Me?

The voice repeated the message three times. Said my name three times. The name I had in the beginning. Norma Jean Baker.

I wondered, should I wait? Resist?

Everything happened very quickly.

I managed to lose weight. I got my original body back. And in the midst of shooting *Something's Got to Give*, I left the world. By my own hand. I flew away._

And then my legend on earth took on new proportions.
Since then, I've been here. At the Gates of Heaven.
I greet.
I listen.
I unite.
I judge.
I speak on His behalf.
I speak about His place.
I'm human. Extraterrestrial. Everywhere. Nowhere. Man. Woman. Neither one or the other. Beyond all borders. All languages.

You see, I'm like you. In misfortune and in power. Divine and orphaned. I'm made of the same stuff as you. I'm in you. In every body. Every night. Every dream.

Don't cry, Jallal.

Take his hand, Mathis.

Go. Go. As brothers of the heart. There, behind that door, life has not even begun for you.

Go. On the way you'll pass a beautiful pomegranate tree. Pick two pomegranates. And later, before you go to sleep, take a moment to eat them.

Come and listen. Downstairs, a mother is getting ready to pray. The echo of her voice will accompany you. It's Mahalia Jackson. She'll start singing *Trouble of the World*.

Listen to her. She speaks the truth. She tells it like it was on the very first day, with the first spark of life. When suddenly, in the infinite, everything exploded and took on new dimensions.

Listen. Listen . . .

> *Soon I will be done*
> *Trouble of the world*
> *Trouble of the world*

Trouble of the world
Soon I will be done
Trouble of the world
Going home to live with God

No more weeping and wailing
No more weeping and wailing
No more weeping and wailing
Going home to live with my Lord
Soon I will be done
Trouble of the world
Trouble of the world
Trouble of this world
Soon I will be done
Trouble of the world
Going home to live with my Lord
I want to see my mother
I want to see my mother
I want to see my mother
Going home to live with God
Soon I will be done
Trouble of the world
Trouble of the world
Trouble of the world
I soon will be done
With the trouble of the world
I'm going home to live with God